THE AMISH SINGLE MOTHER

AMISH MISFITS BOOK 4

SAMANTHA PRICE

AMISH ROMANCE

ISBN: 978-1-5465-8570-1

*J*ane Byler stood by the kitchen table and read her list. Forty-eight plain vanilla cupcakes with assorted frosting colors, fifty-two regular chocolate, all with chocolate frosting, fifty-two pink cupcakes with pink frosting. Letting out a sigh, Jane let the list slip from her fingers. It swayed through the air like an autumn leaf, landing on the wooden table.

"I've told her to order everything by the dozen." All her oven trays were in twelve sections and whenever Miranda gave her an order not divisible by twelve, it led to one thing—larger gas bills. Shaking her head at how Miranda never listened, she picked up a pen and jotted a note to the woman who was giving her the bulk of her work.

To those who knew Jane in the *Englisch* world,

she was known as the cupcake lady. To those in the Amish community, she was little more than an outcast. She wasn't shunned, but the way people avoided her, she might as well have been.

Staying in the community after having a baby out of wedlock was something that was rarely done. The bishop was on her side when she told him what had happened. He knew the real truth, but even after she told her parents, they didn't care. They wanted little to do with her and showed no interest in Tillie, who was approaching her first birthday.

While Jane went through the birth and then the first few months of Tillie's life, she was supported by the charity of the community and now she was solely supported from the sale of her cupcakes. The days were busy up until four p.m. when, every Monday through Saturday, the day's order was collected by Miranda or one of her workers. Then Jane had time to be a regular mom, cook the evening meal and do the daily chores.

Jane had help with the cooking in the afternoons with the cooking in the form of her fifteen-year-old Amish neighbor, Wendy.

Jane looked out the kitchen window at the twinkling stars of the dark night sky. Tillie was in bed and the kitchen was clean, but not all the chores were done—they never were. The cupcakes took priority over chores since they were her sole income. Since her mother didn't visit and neither did anyone else, there was no one to turn their noses up at the undone tasks.

In the stillness of night, while Tillie slept, Jane would sit and plan the next day's baking. Organization was the key to her busy life and she worked better with a prioritized list.

Jane's bottom was just inches off the chair she was about to sit on, and she was ready to start writing that list, when a loud knock on her door startled her. Knowing the sound might wake Tillie if they knocked again, she hurried to see who it was at that late hour. Her first thought was that someone was gravely ill. Her mother or father might've even died. Then again, it could be Wendy to see if she was needed the next day, but Wendy never knocked.

After she had flung open the door, her eyes adjusted to an unexpected, yet not totally unpleasant sight. A tall Amish man stood before her, smiling. Since the man was a stranger, she pushed the door, so it was only open a crack, and then peeped through. In the dimly lit doorway, she could tell his jaw was square and his features were strong. *"Jah?"*

"Jane?"

She looked him up and down. His white shirt was barely tucked into his trousers and his suspenders appeared to be striped—an odd choice for an Amish man. No, he was no one she knew, she was certain of it. *"Jah,* I'm Jane."

"I'm Adam's *grosskin."* He looked at Jane as though she should know him. When she remained silent, he added, "My *grossdaddi* is Adam Fisher … from next door." He jolted his head to one side, attempting to point to Adam's house behind him with his head.

"Oh, you're Adam's *grosskin?"*

The young man smiled. "That's right. I arrived here this afternoon and I just wanted to introduce myself. And you're Jane …?"

Jane wasn't happy about him being there after dark. It was inconsiderate, especially since she had a young child. He could've come there earlier or waited until the next day. She looked down at the ground. "It's late."

"I know. I hope I'm not disturbing you. It's just that I wonder if you might have any *kaffe* that I could borrow? Just a small amount?"

"Why?"

He breathed out heavily and an embarrassed smile met his lips. It was then she noticed the dimples in his cheeks. "Because if you do, I'll ask if I

4

can borrow some. I'll replace it tomorrow." When she remained silent once again, he continued, "I always start my day with a cup of *kaffe* and I noticed that Adam doesn't have any, so—"

"Wait right there." Jane closed the door and hurried to get the stranger some coffee. If he kept talking, he might wake Tillie and then her peace and her routine would be out the window. On opening the cupboard, she saw instant coffee, ground coffee, and coffee beans. If Adam didn't have coffee in the house, she reasoned, he wouldn't have a coffee grinder. Reaching in, she grabbed the jar of instant and hurried back to her unwanted guest. She opened the door just enough to allow the jar of coffee and a hand through. "There."

"*Denke.* I'll bring it back tomorrow."

"*Nee*, don't!" When he looked at her, shocked, she realized how abrupt she'd sounded. "It's okay, it's fine. You can keep it." She closed the door on him.

"It was nice to meet you, Jane with no last name," he said through the closed door.

Rolling her eyes, she walked back to the kitchen. As soon as he heard the rumors about her, he wouldn't think it was nice to meet her. He'd be avoiding her just like the rest of them, which was partly why she'd avoided the use of her last name.

Old Adam next door had been fine to her, but he didn't know what was going on around him most of the time.

~

THE NEXT MORNING, Jane was on top of things and running according to schedule. Tillie and she had eaten breakfast and now Tillie was down for her morning nap. The first batch of cupcakes was in the oven and just about cooked. She'd finished mixing the second batch, when a knock sounded on the door. Jane opened it, expecting to see the man who delivered her weekly groceries running extra early.

Adam's grandson stood there smiling and holding a jar of coffee.

She looked down at the unopened jar. "That's not mine. That's new."

"I know. I went to the store first thing and bought you a new jar."

"If you were going to the store first thing, why didn't you buy a take-out *kaffe* and then you wouldn't have needed to borrow any last night?"

"Because I like to have a cup as soon as I wake up."

"Keep it," she said, closing the door. Just as she

was walking back into the kitchen, he knocked again. She headed back and swung the door open. *"Jah?"*

His head lowered, but his steely blue eyes were fixed on hers. "Are you sure your name's Jane?"

She wrinkled her nose. He must've heard something about her already. *"Jah,* why?"

"Is there another Jane who lives here?"

"Nee, just me." She frowned at him, slowly losing what little patience she had left.

"My *grossdaddi* told me about the lovely Jane, who lived next door. Do you know where she's gone?"

He was trying to be charming; any other woman would've fallen for it. Even though he was good looking in an obvious way, he was too annoying for her tastes.

No hint of a smile touched her lips, simply because she knew he was trying his best to make her smile. "Your *grossdaddi* and I get along."

"He told me you bake him cupcakes."

"I do, but to be fair, I don't bake them just for him. That's what I do for a living. I bake cupcakes and when I have an odd number I fill the tins with extras, and that's how I have some left over sometimes. He likes them." She shook her head. She was wasting time talking to him when she could be making cakes. That was probably more than she'd spoken to anyone for the whole week.

He tipped his head back and sniffed the air. "Is that something burning?"

"Ach nee!" She raced into the kitchen to see smoke rising from the cracks of the oven door. With no time to pull on her oven mitts, she held them over her hands, opened the oven, and pulled out the tray. She turned around to see if there was a clear space to dump the tray somewhere and she got such a fright to see that the man had followed her inside, she lost her grip on the tray. As it fell, she tried to steady it and burned her hand. She let out a yowl.

CHAPTER 2

*H*e rushed to her. "Your hand."

"Please leave the *haus*." She grabbed a tea towel, and bent down to pick up the pan before it made a mark on her linoleum flooring. "They're ruined," she muttered, fighting back tears. Every cent she made was for Tillie's and her future. She couldn't afford mistakes like this.

"Are you okay?"

"*Nee*, I'm not," she spat out. "I've burned my hand too."

He whipped around to the tap and turned it on. "Quick, put it under here."

"It'll be okay. I burn myself all the time. It's a hazard of the job." She dumped the tray on the large sheet of metal that covered most of the table. *Why hasn't he gone yet?* She didn't want to be too rude to the man since Adam had always been good to her.

"Under here." He spoke with such force it startled her and she looked up at him in shock. He gave a small smile. "It'll make it better. Trust me."

She turned, switched off the oven, and then stuck her hand under the cool running water. Turning her hand over, she saw the angry red mark that stung so badly.

He stepped back a bit while she glanced over at the black cupcakes.

"This isn't a good sign," she said.

"What's that?"

"When the day starts out like this, it just gets worse. I've lost time and I hope the rest of the cakes won't smell of smoke. There would be nothing worse."

"*Jah*, smoked fish is tasty, but I don't think I'd fancy smoked cake. How many do you make a day?"

"It varies, but mostly one hundred and forty four. I supply a caterer and she also owns a restaurant."

"And is that all you do?"

She looked at him open-mouthed, wondering if she'd heard correctly. "And where would I find time to do anything else? That's a lot of cupcakes. It takes me all day. It's not just the baking. It's the packaging and the frosting, and also the decorating."

He glanced at her oven. "If you had a bigger oven, it wouldn't take you as long. Surely it would be more cost-effective too."

"I know that!" she snapped before she caught herself. "You're right. That's what I'm saving for." She twisted her body to stare at him. "What did you say you're visiting Adam for?"

"The rest of the family is worried about him."

"Are they worried because he's leased this *haus* to me? Do they want me to pay more? Is that why you're here? I guess I can manage more, but he could've asked me himself. They didn't need to send you."

He laughed. "Relax. It's not about you. It's his *haus.* He can do what he wants with it. *Nee,* they're worried about him. He never writes or calls anymore, so they sent me to stay for awhile."

"They sent you?" She turned the tap off.

"Leave it on for longer." He moved forward and turned the tap back on. "*Jah,* they sent me." Once she had her hand back under the water, he looked around about him. "Do you live here by yourself?"

"I've got Tillie, my *dochder.*"

He glanced over at the dining room off from the kitchen, which Jane had fixed with a gate to make a large playpen. "How old is she?"

"She's nearly one."

"Did your husband die?"

"You ask a lot of questions. We've only just met." As annoying as he was, he was someone to talk to and she hadn't had many of those of late.

He laughed. "I'm sorry. Do you have ice?"

"What for?"

"Your hand."

She turned off the cold water. "It should be okay now."

"You should look after it."

"I don't have time. I've got cupcakes to bake and it's easier for me if I do as much as I can before Tillie wakes. So, I'm sorry to sound rude, but you'll have to leave."

"Okay. I'm sorry about your cupcakes."

"Me too."

On his way out, he looked over his shoulder at her as she followed right behind him. "Shouldn't you use a timer?"

She was tempted to say something rude, or throw something at him, but she managed to calm herself.

"Normally I don't need one because people aren't knocking on my door so early in the morning."

He chuckled. "I don't see why not."

"If you stay here any length of time, you'll find out why."

Once he was at the front door, he turned to face her. "Why? Is there something wrong with you?"

She opened the door wide and gestured with her hand for him to leave. "There's nothing wrong with me."

"What will I find out if I stay here long enough?"

"I don't know. I've got no idea what they say about me behind my back." That wasn't quite true; she had a pretty good idea.

"Have you got something in those cupcakes that makes you paranoid?"

She fixed her hands on her hips. "There's nothing in my cupcakes. They're perfectly good."

"Calm down. I didn't mean you had anything in your pancakes."

"They're cupcakes!"

"I meant cupcakes. I don't know why I said pancakes. I must be hungry."

"Well go and cook yourself some pancakes, Adam's nameless *grosskin*."

"Maybe I will, Jane with no last name."

"Fine. You do that." She closed the door on him, hoping he hadn't been hinting for her to make him breakfast. Jane headed back to the kitchen, figuring that the best way to get rid of the smoke was to leave the oven door open and open the windows.

Once she threw out the charcoal-black cakes, she gave the warm oven a wipe down with a damp cloth. Feeling her angry wound stinging, she turned to the sink and let the cold water wash over it once more.

This was a setback, but she was used to those.

When there was another knock on the door, she headed back out, hoping it wasn't Adam's grandson again. It wasn't. The delivery man, Joe, was there with her weekly food order.

Jane had sourced the best ingredients at the lowest prices at a bulk wholesale rate and the firm had agreed to free delivery. The eggs came fresh from the chickens next door, gathered by Wendy and kindly left at her door in the early hours of the morning.

When Joe had gone, she glanced over at Adam's house and wondered how long his handsome grandson was staying. If the family was so worried about Adam, why hadn't they taken him to live with them?

The rest of the day she spent angry with Adam's grandson for being the cause of her ruined batch of cakes and her burned hand. Walking right into her house the way he'd done was just unforgivable.

CHAPTER 3

*J*ane always baked the cakes as early in the day as she could, so they'd be cooled and ready for the decorating phase that took place later in the day.

Jane peeped into Tillie's room. Her daughter normally never cried when she woke. "Hello, my *boppli.* You're awake already. I'll change your diaper and give you something to eat." She leaned down and picked her up.

"Mamma." As Tillie normally did, she reached for the strings of Jane's prayer *kapp*, pulling them into her mouth before Jane could move them away.

"*Nee*, Tillie. I told you not to do that."

When Tillie had undergone a diaper change, Jane placed her in the highchair and they both had lunch. It was early for most people to have the midday meal, but with their early start, it made sense for them to eat just before eleven. Everything had to be run according to a routine for Jane to produce the cakes on time.

When they'd finished eating, Tillie was placed into her large playpen area and Jane went back to work.

Movement outside the window caught her eye and she looked out to see Adam's grandson walking from his grandfather's house to hers with something in his hands.

Jane sighed loudly. "What now?" There was no time designated to answer the door to unwanted guests. Just as well she didn't have anything in the oven this time. She opened the door just as he was walking up the porch steps.

"Hello." Dimples appeared in his cheeks when he smiled.

"Look, I don't want to be rude or unfriendly, but I'm very busy all through the day. I explained to you earlier that I work here at the *haus.*"

"I know you're working."

"I've heard people don't respect your time when you work from home. They think they can stop by at any time, but they wouldn't do it if I worked in an office. Would you?"

He frowned and his smile was gone. "Would I what?"

"Would you stop by like this if I was working in an office?"

"*Nee*, because my *grossdaddi* doesn't live next to an office building." He flashed her a beaming smile.

His cute act was good, but he was wasting his time on her. She folded her arms across her chest. "Do you want something?"

"*Nee.* I came to give you this." He held out a white box.

Since he held it out, she took it from him, and once it was in her hands, she noticed it was light. "What is it?"

"It's a cake."

She didn't believe she'd heard correctly. "Excuse me?"

"A cake."

"You brought *me* a cake?"

He nodded, grinning widely.

"I look at cake all day. Why would you give me a cake?"

"As a peace-offering. We got off to a bad start."

She shook her head, staring at the box.

"I ... I couldn't think of what else to bring." His smile was gone and he looked down.

"Anything but cake."

"It's red velvet."

"Look, that's really nice of you and I can tell you're a nice young man, but—"

His sudden laughter startled her. "Nice young man? No need to be condescending. I'm older than you. I just wanted to do something nice. You seem to be going through a tough time."

"I don't need anyone to be nice to me."

"I said, *do* something nice for you. Shouldn't you expect everyone to be nice to you?"

"Look, you're new here and you don't know how things work." Time was ticking away and talking to Adam's grandson wasn't making her money. She had to get rid of him and get back to work. Now Tillie wailed because she was used to seeing her mother in the kitchen when she was in her play-area. "I'm coming, Tillie," she called over her shoulder.

"Is that your *dochder?*"

"*Nee*, it's a puppy I've trained to sound like a young child." Now she felt bad for being so rude. "I'm sorry. I didn't mean to say that. I do have to go and get on with the baking." She offered him back the cake by way of extending it toward him.

"You don't want the cake?"

When she held it out further, he had no choice but to take it from her.

"It's a lovely thought and I appreciate it. Your *grossdaddi* will eat it."

"I'm sorry to bother you, Jane." He took a step back, and said under his breath, "Jane with no last name."

"I have to go." She closed the door and headed back to the kitchen. "It's okay, Tillie, *Mamm's* back. We had a visitor, but he's gone. He was a really annoying one, but he eventually left. He brought us cake. Can you believe that? Wendy will be here later to help us."

"Mamma," Tillie mumbled as she played with the toy cupboard once full of plastic bowls and spoons that were now scattered on the floor around her.

After Jane measured out the flour into the sifter, she moved forward to look out the window at Adam's grandson. She still didn't know his name. He said he was older, but how would he know how old she was? Perhaps he was in his mid twenties, so it was reasonable for him to think he was older. Jane felt a lot older than her twenty years after everything she'd been through with the unexpected pregnancy, the outrage from a segment of the community who didn't know the truth, and her family all but disowning her.

The bishop had announced at one of their meetings that Jane was not shunned due to certain circumstances. She'd asked him not to tell everyone she'd been raped, not wanting Tillie to know she'd been born from violence. Many people had guessed what had happened, although no one except the few people Jane had told knew for sure.

Fixing her eyes on the man's back, she noticed an air of confidence about him. It was odd to have someone be so friendly with her, but she didn't need his attention.

CHAPTER 4

*A*t two o'clock, Wendy rushed into the kitchen—she never knocked.

"Did you see him?"

Jane looked up. "Who?"

"Japheth. He's staying with Adam next door. Someone said he's Adam's *grosskin*."

"Ah, that's his name. *Jah*, I saw him. He came here and made me burn my cakes and my hand early this morning." Jane held up her hand to show her young friend.

"Ouch!"

"It still hurts. It could've been worse, I suppose."

"Is he really as handsome as they say?"

Jane narrowed her eyes. "Who was talking about him?"

"Everyone. Well, all the girls. They say he's got

big brown eyes and dark hair, he's tanned, and he's got the broadest shoulders."

Jane shrugged. "His eyes are blue."

Wendy whipped her head around to stare into Jane's face. "Ah, blue, are they, *jah*?"

"*Jah*."

"So, you noticed his eyes?"

"I'm not interested in him, if that's why you're smirking like that. I just notice people's eye-color, that's all."

"Hmm. Anyway, what do you think of him?"

He was, she thought, the type of man girls would like. It was a wonder he wasn't taken already. "He's alright. He's friendly."

"Is that all?"

"I guess he's handsome."

"I can't wait to meet him."

Jane concentrated on piping the frosting onto the cake in front of her while her friend stood staring. It was an art she'd perfected to get it just so. Wendy was a wiz at decorating the cakes—arranging the sprinkles and extras—and that allowed Jane to get on with more of the piping. Wendy didn't have the knack to pipe the frosting just yet and needed more practice.

When Tillie gave a few whimpers, Jane looked at

the clock. "Do you mind giving her a bottle and putting her down for her nap?"

"Sure, I'd be happy to."

Several minutes later, Wendy reappeared in the kitchen. "She's nearly asleep."

"*Denke,* Wendy. She'll be asleep soon. It never takes her long."

"Well, what do you think about Japheth? You've hardly told me anything about him."

"He seems nice. There's not really much to tell apart from him being the cause of my burn."

"I've been praying that you'll meet a man, so Tillie can have a family, with a *Mamm* and a *Dat.*"

Jane chuckled. "Really? That's kind." Wendy was full of youthful naivety, and Jane hoped that would never have to change. "Tillie and I are our own family. All I'm doing is making a decent life for Tillie and me. If the perfect man came along, I wouldn't turn him away, but looking for a man isn't in my plans."

Wendy gasped. "Why not?"

"It's easier that way, that's all. You know what my life's like. A man would hardly fit in. And if I ever got married, how do I know that he and his family would treat Tillie well?"

"Why wouldn't they?"

"I don't want to talk about it anymore. You can talk about Japheth or anyone else you want, but don't talk about me with a man. Okay?"

Wendy nodded. "I won't. What would you like me to do now?"

Jane glanced at the clock once more. Miranda would be there in an hour. "We've got one hour to get these finished and boxed before Miranda gets here. You decorate them as I frost them."

Jane had set four extra cakes onto the oven trays to take over to Adam and his grandson when she was done with the day's work. She hadn't meant to be so hostile to Japheth when he was only being friendly; she regretted her rudeness. Since some of the day's order was for mini cupcakes, she had spare room on the trays.

~

WHILE THEY WERE HELPING Miranda to the car with the boxes of cakes, Miranda asked, "I've got a full day tomorrow, Jane, so would you mind just this once dropping the order at the restaurant?"

"That's not part of the deal."

"Just this once? I've got two workers on vacation, and the rest of the staff will be needed at the restaurant tonight full-time. I'm sorry, but I can't spare one of them to drive out here. I thought you wouldn't mind. I'll pay the taxi fare, of course. Please?"

Miranda had never asked her before. "Okay then," Jane agreed. Besides keeping Miranda happy, it would be a good reason for her and Tillie to get out of the house. She hadn't been anywhere in so long.

Miranda patted her on the shoulder. "Thanks so much, Jane. I appreciate it." Miranda got into her car and sped down the driveway.

"Where do you have to take the cupcakes?" Wendy asked, having been too far away to fully hear what was said.

"To her restaurant."

"That explains it. She owns a restaurant and she does catering?"

"*Jah.* I thought you knew that. I worked in her restaurant when I was on *rumspringa.*"

"Yeah, I knew that, but I didn't know the other thing. No wonder she always seems in a hurry."

Jane sighed as they walked back up the porch steps. "I'd like to own a little business, a store somewhere, one day."

"You will. And I'll be one of your workers."

"Absolutely. I'd hire you in a heartbeat."

Wendy giggled. "Tomorrow's Saturday. Do you want me here early, so we can start and finish early?"

"*Denke.* And I must pay you more if you're spending all Saturday here when you could be with your friends."

"I don't want any more than normal. Just give me a job when you open your restaurant. Anyway, I'm spending Saturday afternoon and Saturday night with my friends."

"Are you sure your parents don't mind you being here so often?"

"They don't mind. They like you, and they hardly notice I'm gone."

CHAPTER 5

*J*ane placed Tillie in her high chair, lined up all the vegetables on the table, and then sat down next to Tillie to peel them. Tillie bounced up and down, trying to get one of the carrots. "Hold on. I'll cut you one."

She handed her daughter a strip of carrot and chewing on that kept her occupied. As Jane peeled the vegetables, she thought back over her day, and how she'd treated Japheth. Her newly-developed bad temper was something she didn't like, and she always felt dreadful after every outburst. She'd even been a bit short with Miranda. She looked over at Tillie who was happily working her new bottom tooth into the carrot.

"Let's take those cupcakes over to them soon. After I cook our vegetables and fry our meat." Tillie smiled at her as though she'd understood every word.

It was just getting dark when she and Tillie were ready to take over the cupcakes to Japheth and Adam. Tillie had been bathed and was ready for bed. "I'll take you over to visit Adam and his grandson and then it's into bed for you. Okay?"

Her baby stared up at her, babbling a 'Tillie-talk' reply.

With Tillie on her hip and a plate of cupcakes in the other hand, she made her way to Adam's house. When she got to the front door, she found she didn't have a spare hand to knock. "Hello," she called out.

A few seconds later, Japheth opened the door. "This is a surprise."

"This is *my* peace offering," she said, handing him the plate of cakes. It was then she remembered that he already had a red velvet cake, so it seemed a little weird to be bringing him more cake. He was too polite to point that out.

His face lit up as he stared at them. "Wow! These are your famous cupcakes?"

"They are."

He placed his hand on his chest. "For me?"

"Well, for you and for Adam."

"Come in."

"Oh no, I've got to put Tillie to bed. I didn't mean to bother you, or anything."

He stepped back. "You're here now, so come inside. Hello, Tillie," he said as Jane stepped inside.

"She can't talk yet. She says some form of language and it's all mumbles. Maybe she knows what she means." Jane giggled. When she walked further inside, she saw Adam asleep on the couch. He was in a seated position with his head back and his mouth wide open. "*Ach nee.* I'm sorry," she whispered. "I shouldn't have been talking so loudly. Why didn't you tell me Adam's asleep?"

"Don't worry, he's a sound sleeper. Come through to the kitchen."

She followed Japheth into the kitchen where she smelled the dinner cooking. "Are you having a roast?"

"Correct. Would you like to stay?"

"*Nee denke.* We've already eaten. Did you cook or did Adam?"

"Adam's been asleep for the past hour. I cooked. I quite enjoy cooking."

"I didn't realize."

He glared at her so hard his brow furrowed. "I don't look like the type of man who could cook, or you didn't realize that a man could cook?"

Jane couldn't keep the smile from her face at the way he pretended to be offended. "I guess so. Maybe both, or all three, I mean. Most of them can't."

"It's not that difficult."

"You're right. It's not."

"But too difficult for a man?"

Jane laughed, realizing he was acting like the male version of her.

He placed the plate of cupcakes on the table and looked at her. "What's so funny?"

"Nothing." She coughed and made a serious face. "I should've brought you cupcakes another night when you didn't have the red velvet cake to eat as well."

"You can't have too much cake in the *haus*, that's what I always say. Have a seat." He quickly turned, leaned over, and checked on the food in the oven.

She sat down at the kitchen table and placed Tillie on her lap.

When he closed the oven, he sat down opposite her. "How's your hand?"

Lifting her arm above the table, she showed him. "It still hurts, but I'll live."

He grimaced. "It looks sore."

Jane nodded. "Yeah. Anyway, what did you do today?"

"Not much. Just talked with Adam and did a few repairs around the place. I know what you were doing."

"*Jah*, I'm always busy, except on Sundays"

"It was nice of you to make us the cupcakes. I'm looking forward to tasting one. I won't have one now, or I'll spoil my dinner." He drummed thoughtfully on the table with his fingertips. "I wonder where that rule came from."

"What rule?"

"The rule where you can't have sweet things before you eat the main meal."

"Hmm. That's a good point. I think sweet things fill you up and then you don't want to eat your vegetables."

"*Jah.* You're probably right. Spoken like a *mudder.*"

"*Jah.* I am one."

"You've all got the same *mudder* rules."

When he smiled, she saw how truly handsome he was. He had the perfect shaped masculine face and his nose wasn't too big or too small. She pushed out her chair. "I should be going."

"So soon? Can't you stay and talk to me for a bit?"

"Um, okay, just for a few more minutes." She sat down again.

"Tell me about your family." He fixed his eyes on her.

"There's not much to tell. I'm the youngest of seven. The eldest two are girls and the rest are boys, until me. They're all married and have *kinner*. What about you?"

"We have something in common. I'm the youngest as well, the youngest of five. All boys. *Mamm* always wanted a girl, but she didn't get one."

"All your *brieder* are married?"

"*Jah,* the closest one to me in age just got married last month."

She nodded, trying to look interested, but she wasn't, not really. Small talk was something she'd never been good at. She was pleased when Tillie started crying. "I really should go. Tillie's getting tired."

He stood as well. "Is she ready for bed?"

"*Jah.* This is bedtime for her."

He walked her to the front door and, on the way, she glanced over to see Adam still asleep.

"*Denke* for stopping by, Jane, and for bringing cake. You and cake are always welcome."

Just as she walked out the door, she turned around. "Enjoy the cupcakes."

"I'm sure I will."

She took two steps away.

"Oh, Jane."

She spun back around. *"Jah?"*

"You and Tillie should come for dinner one night."

"Yeah, maybe."

"I'll cook something special. I'll look up Adam's recipe index cards."

Jane giggled, knowing Adam didn't have recipe cards; Japheth was being silly. "Okay. One night—maybe." She walked faster when Tillie made whimpering sounds.

CHAPTER 6

The next day, Jane was half expecting Japheth to stop by, but there had been no sign of him. She and Wendy were ahead of schedule with the cakes. Wendy had offered to watch Tillie while Jane delivered the cupcakes to Miranda's restaurant, but Jane wanted to take her daughter into town with her. They would have something to eat at a café and enjoy getting out of the house for a change.

Two of Miranda's staff members helped get the cakes out of the taxi while Jane headed inside to collect the money from Miranda.

"Miranda's in the back if you want to see her," one of the staff said as she passed by.

"Thanks." Jane pushed Tillie in her stroller, heading to Miranda's back room. Miranda was busy talking with someone when she pushed the door open.

"Oh, I'm sorry," Jane said, taking a step back and closing the door.

Miranda met her outside the office. "What do I owe you today, Jane?"

Jane handed her the invoice and the stub from the taxi driver.

Miranda took it from her, walked back into her office, and then reappeared with the money.

"Thanks, Jane. I really appreciate you bringing this in. I won't ask again. We've just got so much going on here tonight. You don't want your old job back, do you?"

"What? And leave you with no cupcakes? No."

Miranda laughed. "Bye, Jane."

After she had said goodbye to Miranda, she pushed the stroller through the restaurant and back onto the busy street. Tillie was quiet because she loved going for walks in the stroller.

Jane headed further up the street, stopping every now and again to look in store windows. When someone tapped on her shoulder, she turned around and looked into the eyes of the person she feared most in the world. It was the man who'd assaulted her. She'd heard he'd moved to New York otherwise she never would've gone into town.

"Leave me alone." She backed away, stepped aside, and pushed the stroller away from him.

"Wait up, Jane."

"Go away."

She heard footsteps and then he leaped in front of the stroller and she couldn't move.

"Wait up! You went back to the Amish?"

"Obviously."

His gaze dropped to Tillie and then he eyed Jane suspiciously. "How old is he?"

"None of your business, and he's a she."

He looked back down at Tillie. "Is that my kid?"

"Don't be ridiculous. Now get out of my way, or I'll scream."

He didn't move a muscle. Instead, he crouched down to Tillie's eye-level and looked into her face. "She looks just like my brother's kid."

"All kids look the same. Move out of my way." Jane looked around, hoping against hope that there would be a police officer nearby, but the street had become strangely deserted. When he moved out of her way, she started walking off, but he grabbed her arm and dug his fingers in so hard she yelped in pain.

"I reckon that's my kid."

"She's not," Jane snapped. "I told you already."

"Whose is it then?"

She stared into his hateful eyes. "None of your business."

He chuckled. "That's what I thought."

She didn't want to speak to him, but she had to know whether she could come back into town again. "Didn't you move away?"

"I just got back yesterday. I kind of like the idea of being a father now my brother's got a kid. Can't let him get one up on me with my folks. This news'll make my parents happy and I reckon this kid'll help me get back into their will." He laughed.

A shiver ran down her spine. His parents were influential and wealthy. That was one reason she had never reported the rape. He'd told her that no one would believe her and that his parents had more than enough money to hire the best lawyers.

"Then you'll look a complete fool when they find out she's not yours."

"Somehow, I don't think that'll happen."

As soon as he released her arm, she pushed the stroller as fast as she could away from him.

"If you don't want to share, I'll be happy to take her from you," he called out.

She made no comment and didn't look back. Even if he tried to take her away, Jane was sure it wouldn't happen. Not when she'd raised Tillie these first twelve months of her life. It was only six blocks later when she slowed down and saw a café. A quick look behind her told her she hadn't been followed.

After wrestling the stroller through the doors of the coffee shop, she sat down at one of the tables, got Tillie out of her stroller, and held her tight in her arms. "No one's taking you away from me."

"Joos."

Jane laughed at Tillie trying to say 'juice.' "You can have some juice. You can have whatever you want."

When she saw a figure in front of her, she said, "I'll have an apple juice and I'll have a …" She looked up to see it wasn't a waiter at all.

41

She was relieved that it was Japheth from next door who was standing there, looking down at her. "Oh, it's you."

"Mind if I sit?"

She nodded, secretly glad to see someone friendly after running into Scott Crittenden. "Please do."

"Did I hear you say you wanted an apple juice?" he asked.

She managed a smile. "For Tillie. She loves apple juice."

"I'll get it. What would you like?"

"*Nee*, that's okay. I'll get it. What would you like?"

He shook his head. "Allow me. As an apology for being silly enough to buy you that red velvet cake."

"*Denke.* Just a hot tea for me."

"Anything to eat?"

She shook her head. "I'm not hungry."

"I won't be a minute."

Jane put Tillie back in her stroller.

Japheth sat back down a few minutes later and placed a number on the table. "Now, what's got you looking so upset? You didn't burn more cakes, did you?"

"What are you doing here?" Jane asked, avoiding his question with one of her own.

"I was having a look around the town and I saw you talking to someone and then you ran away from him. Did he upset you?"

She narrowed her eyes. "You followed me here?"

"You looked upset."

Jane hadn't seen anyone when she looked around. "I didn't see you when I was talking to him. Where were you?"

"I was at the post office across the road."

Shaking her head, she said, "He's a dreadful person."

"I kind of figured that, the way you were trying to get away. What did he do to make you so upset?"

She shook her head. "It doesn't matter now. It's all in the past. Anyway, are you going to the young people's thing on tonight? Wendy was telling me that there was something on."

He shook his head. "I'm a little old to be included in the young people's 'things.'"

"Exactly how old are you?"

"Twenty-eight, and five months and … and seven days. Exactly."

She laughed, and said, "Oh, I didn't think you would be *that* old. I thought you were twenty-two, or twenty-three, or something."

"And I'm guessing you're around twenty, although you act like you're forty."

Jane lowered her gaze to the red and white checkered tablecloth. Then she looked back into his deep blue eyes. "That's how I feel sometimes. I'm a *mudder* now, and trying to make ends meet."

"You say that as though your life's over."

"I didn't mean it to sound like that. I love being a *mudder*."

He scratched his neck. "If you don't mind me asking, Adam told me you're not that close with your *familye*. Adam said they're in the community and don't live far away, and they don't help you out."

"My *familye* and I don't see eye-to-eye about many things. It's just me and Tillie now."

"You and Tillie against the world?"

"Not really. I've got some good friends in the community. Wendy's family, and the bishop and his family have always been good to me. They saw to it I had enough money to get by before I started cooking for Miranda." He continued to stare at her, which made her uneasy, so she kept talking. "Anyway, how's Adam? Have you achieved what you've come here to do?"

"Wait a minute. Was that guy back there threatening you about something?"

"*Jah*, he was."

He shook his head. "I didn't realize."

"What would you have done if you had?"

"I would've told him to leave you alone."

Jane shook her head. "He's a dangerous person."

"I'm sorry, Jane. I'm pretty thick in the head sometimes."

Jane gave a little giggle and then was distracted by Tillie trying to undo the strap that kept her safely in her stroller. "Stay there, Tillie."

"There's a highchair over there. Want me to grab it?"

She glanced around to where he was looking. "*Jah*, please."

He leaped up and while he was gone, Jane unstrapped Tillie and held her in her arms. When he brought the chair over to the table, she lowered Tillie into it. The chair didn't have any straps and Tillie was a squirmer, so Jane pulled the chair closer to her.

"Anyway, you were asking me if I'd achieved what I'd set out to do here."

"Have you?" Jane asked.

"You want me to go already? I thought you'd want me to stay a bit longer since we've become friends."

"Friends? Is that what we are?"

"We're sitting down together. We must be. We're both too old to go to young people's things—you're old in the head, anyway—and we don't fit into the young marrieds scene because we're not married. It makes sense we'd become friends. We've got so much in common."

Jane smiled at him and found she was enjoying his company. He was unlike any man from her community. "I'm even more odd because I have a child. At least it's respectable to be single and child-less. I don't fit—"

"Jane, you are respectable and you shouldn't think otherwise."

"I know I am." It was others who didn't think she was. "I didn't quite mean it like that."

"Good."

The waitress brought apple juice, coffee, and tea to the table.

"Thank you," Japheth said.

"Your toasted sandwiches won't be long."

"How many are you having?" Jane asked when the waitress left.

"I'm having one and you're having one. I'll share with Tillie if she wants some."

"I'm not hungry and Tillie won't be hungry either. She ate just before we left home."

"Well, all the more for me then." He shook his head. "You make it hard."

"What?"

"You make it hard to be friends with you."

"I'm sorry. I don't mean to be so horrible. It's just that I'm out of practice being around people. I go to the meetings, but I keep to myself most of the time. Not many people talk to me and I've given up trying to talk to them. I have to warn you, I'm an outcast. You might be too if you're seen with me."

"*Jah*, you keep telling me that. You don't fit what people think you should be. I'm an outcast too."

Jane laughed. He was handsome, and all the girls were talking about him, according to Wendy. He was anything but an outcast. "Why would you say that?"

He looked up. "I'm misunderstood." When his lips twisted into a smile and she saw his dimples, she knew he was poking fun at her.

"I don't know if you truly belong. It's an exclusive club."

"I noticed."

She leaned toward him. "Haven't you heard talk about me yet?"

He leaned further forward until his face was two inches away from hers. "*Nee.*"

Jane drew back. "Really?"

"Perhaps you're not as interesting to others as you think."

"It's not that—"

"Drink your hot tea before it goes cold."

Jane looked at her tea, frowning as he picked up his coffee. It had been a while since someone had told her what to do. She took a quick sip and then poured juice into Tillie's empty bottle. Tillie grew excited watching her juice be poured and banged on the tray of her highchair, causing Japheth to jump.

Laughing at him, Jane passed the bottle to Tillie. "Are you scared of *bopplis*?"

"Sometimes, I guess. I haven't had much to do with them. Two of my brothers have *kinner*, but I can't get near them. They're younger than Tillie, and my *schweschder*-in-laws don't let anyone near them."

"Why's that?"

He shook his head. "Overprotective, I guess."

"I was like that for the first few months. I think I got over that when she started crawling and putting everything she could into her mouth."

The waitress put two plates of toasted sandwiches on their table. "Are you waiting on anything else?"

"No, thank you."

The waitress took their order number off the table.

"Maybe I could have a little bit," Jane said, suddenly feeling hungry.

"Sure." He pushed one plate toward her. "Cheese and tomato. What could be better on a day like today?"

Jane ignored his prattle and noticed Tillie's gaze was fixed on the food. She broke off a crust and handed it to her. Tillie eagerly took it from her and started chewing on it.

"She looks hungry now," Japheth said.

"*Jah*." Jane said, "or just interested to try something new."

"Anyway, what are you doing in town? You told me you never get out and never go anywhere."

"I don't usually. The lady I bake the cupcakes for said she had no way of collecting them today, so I drove them here in a taxi."

"I could've driven you. I've got the use of Adam's buggy."

"I couldn't have asked. Anyway, it didn't occur to me."

"While I'm here, you should take advantage of having an extra friend since you don't have many of them."

She couldn't help but smile. "I'll remember that."

"I'm actually pretty bored. Adam sleeps after breakfast and again early afternoon and I'm not working at all, so there's nothing for me to do."

Jane giggled. "It sounds like he sleeps as much as Tillie."

"Yeah, and he's not nearly as cute. Seriously, though, do you have anything you need done around the place?"

"Mowing my lawn was more than enough help."

"I didn't ... Oh, that's your way of asking me to mow your lawn?"

She smiled, trying not to laugh.

"I'll do it. I'll mow your lawn soon, don't worry about that."

"*Denke.* That would be *wunderbaar.* I always run out of time to do things outside the *haus.*"

"I could plant a garden for you too."

"That's nice of you, but I'd have to look after it, and I wouldn't, and then all the plants would die a horrible death of thirst, or die from strangulation from weeds." She shook her head. "It would be dreadfully slow and awful for them."

"You don't have time to water plants or weed a garden?"

She shook her head. "My life's pretty hectic. It's not easy working from home with a *boppli.* It's two jobs in one. If I had one more thing to do, my stress level would be up to here." She butted the palm of her hand against the top of her forehead.

He drew his eyebrows together. "What about for when Tillie's older? Wouldn't she like a garden to play in?"

"We can plant one together when that time comes."

"Fair enough. I'm pretty good at figures and costings. I helped the family farm save money and I'd reckon if you show me the figures for your business I'd be able to help you make a bigger profit."

It annoyed Jane that he assumed she wasn't already running things well. Was that because she was a woman? *"Denke,* but I've already been over and over the figures."

"A fresh set of eyes could help." He took a large bite of his toasted sandwich.

"Nee denke." Thinking she sounded a little abrupt when he was only trying to be helpful, she added, "I buy the best ingredients at the cheapest possible price and I'm saving to buy a bigger oven. That'll make a difference."

"And you only sell them to the restaurant owner?"

"Jah."

"You'd make more money selling them direct."

"Of course I would, but then I'd have to set something up and pay rent and staff, and all that. It's easier to deal with Miranda. She tells me ahead of time and I make them—simple. Anyway, what do you know about cupcakes?"

"I know if they taste good. The ones you brought over last night were delicious."

"I hope you saved Adam some."

"Nope. He was fast asleep when I ate them. What he doesn't know won't hurt him. Anyway, he'd eaten most of that red velvet cake."

Jane giggled. "You ate them all? You said you were waiting for after dinner."

"Nah. He had one after he woke. And to answer your question, I don't know anything about the food business, but I'm pretty good at numbers. I was just offering to help. That's what friends do."

Seeing Tillie had finished her toast, she broke off another edge for her. Again, Tillie took it eagerly. Jane's mind wandered to Scott and she hoped his threats were empty ones. Surely after what he'd done, he wouldn't be stupid enough to try to take Tillie from her? This was a problem she never thought she'd have to face. After that dreadful episode, Jane had given notice to her flat-mates, and to Miranda, and moved back to her parents' house in the Amish community.

Months later, she discovered she was pregnant and when she told her parents, they sent her to the bishop. She had told the bishop everything and he understood and offered his support. Her mother and her father weren't as understanding and were too worried about her bringing shame upon their good name. Their good name meant more to them than she did. As for the rest of the community, most of them kept their distance.

Jane stared at young Tillie. She'd never treat her

daughter as her parents had treated her. It was unbelievable to Jane that her once loving parents could become so cold and cruel.

Jane took another mouthful of tea. "Is Adam sick or something? Is that why you're here?"

"Well, he's old."

"That doesn't mean he's sick."

He sighed. "I might as well tell you if you can keep a secret." He looked intently into her eyes. "Can you keep a secret, Jane?"

CHAPTER 8

*J*ane nodded. "I can keep a secret, but you don't have to tell me."

"I know I don't." He grunted. "Do you want to know or not?"

She gave a little giggle. "*Jah.* Tell me."

"The truth of why I'm here is that my *mudder* thought it would be good for me to come here to look for a *fraa.*"

Jane giggled and then laughed harder, holding her stomach. The release felt good—just what she needed.

Japheth wasn't smiling. "What's funny?"

She stopped long enough to ask, "Nothing, but couldn't you find one in your own community?"

"*Nee.*"

Gradually, the smile left her face. "I don't think you'll have any trouble."

He ripped off a portion of toast. "I'm not so sure. I've been told I'm too fussy."

"Really? Well, what are you looking for in a *fraa*?"

"I don't think my list is too long."

"You have a list?"

"*Jah.* It's not written down anywhere. It's up here." He tapped his head. "I don't really believe in love, but I figure if I marry at all, she must be beautiful, kind, patient, and nice to animals and old people like my *grossdaddi*."

"Is that it?"

"*Nee*, there's more, but you look bored."

"I'm interested, truly interested. Continue, please." She put her elbow on the table and placed her chin on the edge of her palm.

"Kind—"

"You already said kind. What else do you want?"

He huffed. "I'll know her when I see her."

"So you do believe in love, then, if you'll know her. You believe she exists and she's out there somewhere?"

His dimples once again made an appearance. "To tell you the truth, I haven't thought too much about it."

"But you thought enough about it to create that list."

He frowned at her.

"Come on, tell me what else is on that list."

He chuckled. "You're making fun of me—cruelly mocking me."

"You'd know it if I was. I'm truly interested in what you have to say." Jane knew that he was looking for someone just as handsome as he was. He was probably the perfect man and he was looking for someone equally as perfect. "Start with age. How old would you like her to be?"

He eyed her skeptically. "You really want to know?"

Jane glanced at Tillie to see her staring at Japheth. "Look. Even Tillie wants to know."

He laughed when he saw Tillie staring up at him. "Hypothetically, if I was to marry someone, age is not something that's important. I don't want a young giggly girl, and neither do I want someone who's older than me, or who acts older. It's how old she is in the head that counts. And as well as kind, she must be clever and smart."

"Aren't they one and the same—clever and smart?"

"If you keep interrupting, we won't get home

before dark. I'm not sure how to describe the difference between clever and smart, but they're not the same thing to me. And I haven't asked yet, but do you want me to drive you two home?"

"That would be *wunderbaar, denke*."

His eyes glistened as he spoke again of his ideal woman, explaining exactly how she should be. There were no surprises there. "I'm not sure if I believe in love anyway, after all that. And what about you?" he finally asked. "What are you looking for in a husband?"

"I'm not looking at all."

"Oh, come on. Everyone wants someone." He pushed his dark hair away from his face.

"So you're also a hypocrite? I'm learning so much about you."

"I'm talking theoretically. These things are nice to think about, but in reality is love really what it's cracked up to be?" he asked.

"I can't answer that. Anyway, Tillie and I are fine on our own. I make enough money for both of us, and we're all good." She filled her mouth with the last of the toasted sandwich. When she tried to chew, she realized she should have made it two or three bites, but it was too late. As she chewed, she covered her mouth with her hand.

He drank the rest of his coffee in silence and when Tillie threw her crust on the floor, he picked it up and put it on his own plate. When Tillie grunted with her hand out for the crust, he handed her the bottle of juice.

Jane continued munching on the mouthful, glad he hadn't given Tillie the food from the floor. She'd half expected he would.

"Have dinner with Adam and me tonight."

"*Denke*, that's kind, but maybe another night."

"It's pizza night tonight."

"You're having pizza?" she asked, more interested.

"Yeah, and you said you'd have dinner with us sometime."

She twirled one of the prayer *kapp* strings around her finger. "I thought I said maybe."

"I told Adam I'm bringing pizzas home for dinner. How does that sound? You won't have to suffer through my cooking and pretend to like it."

"That sounds tempting. I like pizzas."

"That settles it. You won't have to cook and there'll be no mess to clean up. You can leave me with all the dishes and go home whenever you feel like it."

She nodded. "*Denke.* I'd appreciate that."

"Try not to let that man bother you. He was probably only full of hot air."

"I really hope you're right."

"Are you ready to go?"

She nodded.

He got out of his chair first and then said, "Are you all right? Do you need any help?"

"*Nee*, it's fine. I'm used to doing everything on my own." She pulled Tillie out of the high chair and put her back into the stroller and buckled her in. Then they headed out of the café.

"My buggy's this way. And I already know where the pizza shop is."

"How do you know that?"

"Adam told me."

While Jane headed to the buggy, she hoped that Scott wasn't spying on her. She glanced around and couldn't see him, but she couldn't shake an awful feeling.

When they got back to Adam's barn, Jane took Tillie home to change her diaper. While she was at her own house, she thought back to the last time she hadn't had to cook dinner. She'd had a couple of meals in the past year at Wendy's house, but that was the only break she'd had. Even though she didn't mind cooking, it was lovely to have a rest from it and from the washing up afterward.

After she had made Tillie a bottle, they headed to Adam's house. There was something about Japheth that attracted her, and she knew she couldn't let that attraction develop. He wouldn't be so attentive if he didn't feel something for her as well. After tonight, she'd keep her distance.

No one deserved to be tied down with someone with her problems. Seeing Scott Crittenden and hearing his threats, Jane knew there were even more problems heading her way. Now that Scott thought Tillie was his, he wasn't going to walk away and forget about it.

CHAPTER 9

Jane normally traveled to the Sunday meetings with either Adam or Wendy's family. Today she chose to go with Wendy's family, figuring it didn't look good to arrive there with Japheth. No doubt if she had, there would've been talk and she didn't want Japheth to be seen with her. It wouldn't give him the best chance of finding a woman, and, because he'd shared his secret with her, she knew that was why he was there.

She arrived before Japheth and Adam, and was sitting at the back of the room when they walked in. There were at least a dozen heads that turned to gawk at Japheth, and most of them were young women. Jane looked away, so he wouldn't see her and do something silly like wave. Jiggling Tillie on her knees, she turned and talked to Wendy.

When the meeting was over, there was the customary meal afterward. Always hoping for reconciliation, Jane took the opportunity to talk to her mother.

Now was a perfect opportunity as her mother was walking away from a lady, having finished a conversation.

"*Mamm.*" Jane's mother stopped still when she saw Jane, and Jane hurried over to her with her daughter in her arms. "That man has come back and says he's going to take Tillie away from me."

"You should have married him. That's what you should've done."

That was the Amish way for anyone who had relations before marriage, but that was not the case in this instance. Why couldn't her mother see that the situation was nothing near the same? "He didn't want to marry me then and he doesn't want to marry me now. And I'd never marry him, no matter what. What you just said is ridiculous!" She licked her lips, aware that her voice was raised; she'd have to control her temper.

Her mother glanced around and then spoke in a low voice. "I'll not talk to you if this is all you want to talk about."

"Don't you want to help me when I'm in trouble?"

"You're old enough to have a *boppli*, so you're old enough to work out your own problems."

"It wasn't my choice. None of this was my choice. The only choice I made was not to have an abortion. What was I to do? This could've happened to anyone."

Her mother just stared at her with cold brown eyes. "There's no point talking about this as though something has changed. Nothing has changed and it never will. You made your decision."

"There's nothing about this that was my decision. What was I to do? What would you have me do?"

"You've always been a stubborn girl." Her mother walked away from her.

Jane didn't blame her, not really. Her mother had toughened her heart against her because the truth of the situation was too awful to face. But Jane didn't have the luxury of looking the other way, or ignoring what had happened. Now she had Tillie, she had to face everything head on. There was no turning her back on the problem or the situation, as her parents and her siblings had done. One older sister, who had moved to a different community, had started writing to her and seemed sympathetic.

She turned back to face the crowd that had gathered around the food tables. A crowd of girls was standing around Japheth in a semi-circle. *That didn't take long.* Jane knew he'd be popular. As she normally did on Sundays, she sat down with Tillie on her lap, somewhere out of the way, and waited until Wendy's family was ready to go home.

~

IT WAS six o'clock in the morning and still pitch black outside. Listening harder, Jane heard the pitter-patter of rain on the roof. She closed her eyes again, enjoying the sound, which had gone from sprinkling to pelting down.

It was then Jane remembered the leak just inside the back door. It hadn't rained for some time and she'd removed the bucket that caught the drips. She switched on the gas lamp next to her and carefully made her way down the steps to the back door.

Her heart sank when she heard the drips landing on the floor before she reached it. By the light of the lamp, she saw there was already water pooling on the floor. With the lamp still in her hands, she used her foot to push the tin bucket from its spot in the corner until it was under the leak. Then she looked up at the wet ceiling.

Adam had been so good to her that she had

delayed telling him about the leak, figuring she'd fix it herself just as soon as she found out how. She left the wet floor, intending to wipe it in the daylight. Catching a few more minutes of sleep was more important right at that moment.

Jane raced back upstairs and slipped between the covers, pleased that the warm spot she'd left was still there.

$$\sim$$

LATER THAT AFTERNOON, Wendy appeared in the kitchen and climbed over the makeshift fence that kept Tillie in the dining room. She picked Tillie up into her arms.

"How was your day, Wendy?"

"I went to Lizzy's house for the quilting bee. I told you I was going there, didn't I?"

"*Jah*, I think so."

Wendy talked so fast and about so many things that Jane lost track of what she was talking about most of the time.

"Anyway, guess what was the topic of conversation?"

"What?" Jane asked.

"Japheth."

Jane's eyebrows rose. "Our Japheth?"

"*Jah*, all the girls are in love with him."

"He's not been here long enough, has he?" Jane asked with a giggle.

"One Sunday meeting. That was enough," Wendy said.

"And what about you? How do you feel about him?"

Wendy shook her head. "What, for you?"

"For you, or for anyone in general."

"He's more suited to you than anyone else. He's more your age."

Jane pressed her lips into a line. "I told you about me and men. It's just not going to happen."

"You've got to get past that. You can't let what happened to you ruin your life."

"I'm past the expiration date for that. A good part of my life has already been ruined. Anyway, all I want now is for Tillie to have a good life. That's all I'm concerned about."

"You've got a long life ahead of you. You could live until you're a hundred; that's another eighty years. Tillie will probably leave home when she's twenty or even younger and then you'll have sixty years alone. *Nee*! Hang on." She held Tillie in one arm while she counted on her fingers. "I think that's right."

"Can't I wait until Tillie leaves home and then think about it?" The idea of Tillie leaving home filled her with horror. But there was a long time to go yet. "Why did you have to say Tillie's going to leave home?"

Wendy laughed. "Everyone leaves their parents' home sooner or later. You did, and I'll leave home soon. Everyone has to leave and start out on their own."

"I know that, but I would rather not think about it."

Worry lines appeared across Wendy's young forehead. "Don't you ever think what it would be like to marry a nice man?"

"I haven't thought about anything like that in a very long time. It's just something that's not going to happen for me. The time for all that has passed me by and I don't even care."

Wendy sat down on the floor with Tillie, and then stacked up all her plastic plates. "Let me know when you need me," Wendy said.

"You've got about ten more minutes."

Jane thought about what her life would've been

like if she hadn't gone on *rumspringa* and hadn't taken that job at that restaurant and gotten to know that terrible man. She most likely would've married one of the Amish men her age. All the men her age were now spoken for and most of them were married. She had no idea which one she would've chosen. There was no one man who'd stood out from the others as being a better match for her than anyone else.

Jane spooned the frosting mixture into the piping bag and then piped the frosting high onto each cupcake. Miranda liked the frosting high, and so did her customers. And piping the frosting was Jane's favorite part of making the cupcakes. When she had one row ready, she called out to Wendy. "I've got some ready for you now."

"Coming." Wendy stood, climbed over the fence, and washed her hands well before she opened the various containers of toppings. "There's no particular themes for these ones?"

"*Nee.* Just do your usual thing."

"You've got no interest in Japheth at all?"

Jane laughed. "He's nice. He's nice to have as a friend and that's all. He's got no interest in me. Put your thoughts into those cakes."

"How could you possibly know that?"

"Know what?" Jane asked.

"You just said he had no interest in you."

"That's right, and I know that from the things we talked about. He said things to me he wouldn't say to me if he was thinking of me as a potential *fraa*."

"Like what?"

"It doesn't matter. Just forget it."

"What? You've got to tell me now."

Jane sighed. "I can't say because he might not want me to repeat it. You know what I mean? I don't want to repeat things and then be accused of gossiping."

"Okay."

"I guess if I was young and carefree and all this hadn't happened to me … I don't really know how I'd feel. I can't turn back the clock so there's no use thinking about it." When they heard a mower start up, Jane smiled. "It looks like I'm about to get my lawn mowed."

"Japheth?"

Jane nodded.

Wendy raised her eyebrows and remained silent.

CHAPTER 10

"*B*ye, Jane. I'll see you tomorrow."

"*Denke* for your help, Wendy. See you tomorrow."

Wendy headed out the back door now that their work was done and Miranda had picked up the order.

With the day having grown cold, Jane headed to the living room and made a fire in readiness for a chilly evening. There was nothing she liked more than drinking a cup of hot tea and staring into the flames after Tillie was in bed. It was therapeutic to do nothing and think of nothing after a hectic day.

As Jane went back into the kitchen, she heard Wendy talking to someone by the back door.

"Japheth's here," Wendy called out.

"Can I come in?" Japheth said from the back door as he knocked.

"*Jah.* Come in," Jane said.

When he didn't appear in the kitchen, Jane looked around the corner to see where he was. He was staring at the bucket of water in the corner. Then he looked up at the ceiling and then he looked at Jane. "What's this?"

"Oh, it's a small leak."

"It doesn't look too small to me."

"It happens every time it rains heavily. I haven't gotten around to fixing it yet."

"I'll get up in the roof and see what's wrong with it."

"*Denke,* and it was good of you to mow the lawn. *Denke* for that too."

"You're welcome. Have you told Adam about the leak?"

"*Nee,* I don't like to bother him. He gives me this place so cheaply; the last thing he'd need would be me complaining about it."

"That's where you're wrong, Jane. He'd want this *haus* to be in good condition. It's not much work to fix a few things here and there, like this leak."

Jane grimaced. "I was worried that it might need a new roof."

He chuckled. "*Nee.* I think the roof is quite good. I'll get a ladder and I'll be back."

"I just opened a bottle of soda. How about a glass of that first and have a sit down before you do anything? I've just lit the fire."

He nodded. "Okay."

As soon as he sat down and had swallowed a mouthful, he started on her. "You really should socialize with people more. I think you're wrong about most people. They're not judging you or thinking bad things about you at all."

"I'm the one who grew up here, remember? I know how people around here think. It's probably different where you come from."

"Once you get to spend time with them, you'll realize how wrong you've been. Avoiding people won't help the situation."

"Here's the problem. I don't fit in with the young marrieds who sit around and talk about their husbands, what their husbands want, how their husbands want their food cooked, and how they're doing this and that for them, so what am I going to talk about? I'm not having any more *kinner*—that's something they talk about all the time too—and I don't have a husband. And then there's the young people's group. I've got Tillie so I can't be one of them. I can't bring her to all the young people's events." She'd told him something of the kind at the café, but like all men it probably went in one ear and out the other.

"You could leave her with someone when you go."

Jane pulled a face. "I don't like leaving her with anyone."

"Or, you can take her to the young marrieds."

She shook her head. "I don't have time for all that. People always think that just because I work from home, I can do anything I want throughout the day. I can't. Right after Tillie and I have breakfast, I cook the rest of the day. I have a break in the middle of the day when the last of the cakes are cooling and then in the afternoon it's frosting, decorating, and packaging. And even at night if I'm not too tired, I get a head start on the next day by creaming the butter and the sugar ready for the morning. Where would I find time to socialize and go to any of these things?"

"I see what you mean. It must be hard."

"It is. Not that I'm complaining. I'm just telling it like it is."

"Who are your friends?"

"There's really only Wendy and her family, and

the bishop's wife, and one of the bishop's daughters, Ruth."

"Is that all?"

"That's all I need. I just told you how busy I am."

He leaned back. "Don't get cranky with me. I was just asking."

"I'm not cranky."

He laughed. "I've heard that girls with red hair have fiery tempers."

She pulled out a strand that had escaped the confines of her prayer *kapp*. "My hair's not red."

Staring at her hair, he said, "I see some red strands there. When you're in the sun it's even more red."

"Oh, I forgot Adam," Jane said, ignoring his intense interest in the color of her hair.

"What?"

"Adam's a friend too."

He drew his eyebrows together. "My *grossdaddi?*"

"*Jah.*"

"Oh good. An eighty-year-old man who sits on the couch and does nothing all day is one of your best friends."

She nodded. "You can think that's funny if you like, but he's done so much for me. He's done more than my family has done for me."

"You mean leasing this house from him?"

"*Jah*. When I was in trouble, he spoke to me at one of the meetings and said his tenants had just moved out. He's letting me rent it for practically nothing. If it weren't for him, I'd have nowhere to live. I'd be homeless. My parents wouldn't have me back."

He shook his head. "I find that so hard to believe."

"It's probably not uncommon."

"That doesn't make it right. Surely the bishop could have a word with your parents about it."

"He probably has for all I know. It's easier to not let it bother me. They've forgotten about me, so I have to forget about them. It makes me more determined to be a better parent to Tillie. And to be kind and compassionate to others." When dimples appeared in Japheth's cheeks, she remembered him continually saying he wanted a kind woman. She cleared her throat. "You better fix that roof before dark."

He rose to his feet as he chuckled. "I don't know if it'll be that easy. I'll be back soon. *Denke* for the conversation and the soda."

Jane bit her tongue to stop herself from telling him, *It wasn't a conversation; it was more of a lecture*, since most of the time he'd been giving her advice.

Tillie was yawning. There was no way she'd make it through to bedtime without falling asleep. She'd already had her two daily naps. If she slept now, hopefully she'd wake up by herself in time for the evening meal, otherwise she'd be one cranky little girl if Jane had to wake her.

Jane had just put Tillie down to sleep when she heard a car pull up outside the house. She pulled aside the curtains in Tillie's room aside and saw Scott Crittenden closing his car door. Frozen in fear, she wondered how he'd found out where she lived. She raced to the door, intent on telling him once and for all to leave them alone.

CHAPTER 11

She flung the door open before he knocked, stepped outside, and quickly closed the door behind her so he wouldn't think he could go inside. "How did you know I lived here?" she spat out.

"It wasn't too hard to find out, especially when I have friends in high places."

"I told you my child has nothing to do with you."

He sniggered while looking her up and down. "I can't believe that."

"Leave now, or I'll call the police."

"No need to get them involved. I'm not doing anything at all, unlike you, keeping my kid from me."

"Leave!"

"I'm going. I just came to give you this." He reached into his back pocket and pulled out a letter and thrust it at her. "And you'll soon get another ordering you to get the kid DNA tested. Mmm, I wonder what that will reveal, eh?"

"You can't do that."

He guffawed. "I did. The ball's already rolling."

She ripped up the letter in front of him and screamed at him. "Go, just go!"

Over his shoulder, Japheth appeared, dropped the ladder by the barn, and hurried over. "Is everything alright, Jane?"

"No, it's not."

"You better go," Japheth called out to Scott Crittenden as he strode toward him.

Scott didn't acknowledge Japheth and kept his cold-hearted eyes fixed on Jane. "You haven't heard the last of this. You can't keep me from her forever. You'd better be careful, or I won't even allow you to see her when I'm granted full custody. My lawyers are doing their research for the case as we speak."

Japheth stepped in between them. "You've upset her enough. It'd be better if you left."

Scott laughed at him and as he did so, Jane balled her hands into fists and charged at Scott, knocking him back as she hit him repeatedly.

Japheth pulled her away. "Come on, Jane. It's okay."

She cried, "It's not okay. It's not!"

Scott backed away, and said to Japheth, "You'd better keep her under control."

When he got into his car, Jane tried to run at him again, but Japheth held on to her. As he drove away, Jane burst into tears.

Japheth still had his arm around her. "What's going on?"

She shook her head. "He's trying to take Tillie away from me."

"He's the father?"

"In name only. Why didn't you let me punch him?" she asked.

"You did." Japheth shook his head. "Violence doesn't get anyone anywhere."

"It made me feel a little better."

"Just calm down." He gestured toward the house. "Go inside out of the cold." With his arm around her shoulder, he walked her into her house. "Sit down on the couch. I'll make you a cup of *kaffe*, or would you like something a bit stronger?"

"I don't have anything strong. I normally don't drink alcohol, but I've got a feeling that's about to change."

"*Kaffe* coming up."

"*Nee*, tea please? *Kaffe* will only keep me awake."

He left her to stare at the fire while he made hot tea. As she stared into the flickering flames, she wondered what would happen now. She looked around for the letter he'd handed her and recalled that she'd ripped it up and left it outside. It was a silly thing, to tear it up. Just as she stood to go outside to retrieve the remnants of the letter, Japheth appeared in the room.

"Where are you going?" he asked.

"I'm just going to see what the letter said."

"What letter?"

"He handed me a letter from a lawyer and I ripped it up and left it outside."

"You stay there. I'll get it." He stared at her intently and pointed to the couch until she sat back down.

Seconds later, the pieces of the letter were in her hands. She pieced it together on the couch beside her. It wasn't from a lawyer like he'd made out; it was just a letter from Scott stating his intentions. He could've told her all that himself, but because he was such a sneaky person she figured there'd be a reason for him giving her that letter.

"What does it say?" Japheth placed a tray on the small table to the side of her. It held a small pot of tea, and a floral-patterned cup and saucer.

"*Denke.* It's not from a lawyer. He probably figured I'd rip it up. It was from him saying he's going to get custody, and he's going to force me to get Tillie DNA tested."

"Why put that in a letter? That wasn't necessary, was it? It seems to me he wanted to see you again."

"Knowing him like I do, there'd be a reason for him handing me this letter. It's probably some legal loophole for him to show the court he's done all the right things and that way he can make out that I'm the bad one."

Japheth sat down opposite her. "Did you know him well?"

"He was a regular at Miranda's restaurant. I worked there for a year when I was on *rumspringa*. He was there nearly every night. He had a friend, a guy called Bonnie, and they'd both stay on after closing and drink with the staff."

"Ah, you knew him reasonably well, then?"

"As well as you ever really know anyone. He asked me out on a date and I was stupid enough to say yes. I thought he was a nice guy; everyone thought he was. He put something in my drink that night and assaulted me. I have vague memories, and that's all." She shook her head.

"I'm so sorry that happened to you."

"*Denke.* It was a long time ago."

"Something like that would stay with you."

"It did and it does. I suppose you heard about that anyway. Have you heard talk about me?"

"Nothing. Don't look so worried."

"Well, wouldn't you be worried if it was all happening to you and someone was now threatening to take your child away—the worst person in the world?"

"Probably, but there must be things you can do about it. He's doing legal things, so perhaps you should get a lawyer."

"I should've kept calm and then told him that there was no way he could take her from me."

"*Jah*, it's always best to remain calm."

"Too late for that now." She grabbed the letter. "His address is here. I should go to his place and tell him calmly that it's not going to happen. He wouldn't risk anyone finding out what really happened. He must be scared I'll say something."

Japheth shook his head. "You should keep your distance. Don't do it."

CHAPTER 12

"*W*hy not?" Jane asked. "If he thinks I'll go to the police, he might back off."

Japheth shook his head. "Don't. It's not a good idea that you go anywhere near him. If you hit him like you just did, he could have you arrested for assault."

Jane gasped. "You're right."

"That would make it easier for him to take legal action against you."

"What should I do?" Jane asked, looking down at the ripped pieces of paper.

"Why don't you write him a letter?"

She looked up at him. "A letter?"

"*Jah*, you can say what you want and you'll have time to think it all over in a calm and cool manner."

89

"You're right. That's a good idea. I'll write a letter. I'll do it tonight and I'll send it tomorrow."

"Good idea. Would you rather be left alone to write or do you want me to hang around a little longer?"

"Please stay awhile. You've got a calming effect on me."

He smiled. "Do I?"

"It's not a compliment. Not that big of a one, anyway."

"Coming from you, I think it is."

Any other time she would've laughed, but that was the last thing she felt like. Again, she looked down at the ripped letter on the couch.

"Drink your tea, Jane. It'll make you feel better."

Her eyes fell to the tray with the empty cup, and the small teapot. *"Denke.* You'll make someone a good *fraa* one day."

"Very funny. Can you just stop making those comments for one moment, and be serious?"

"I will."

He leaned forward, poured the tea into the cup, and carefully passed it to her on its matching saucer.

Jane took the saucer with one hand, and the cup with the other, pleased that he was still there trying to help her. *"Denke.* I'm sorry. I don't know why I keep being mean to you. I'm not an awful person. Well, maybe I am, but I never used to be, at least."

"It's because you're upset and when you're upset, you take things out on those closest to you—your friends."

She grimaced at him calling himself a friend. "Anyway, you gave me some good advice about the letter thing. I'll state all the facts clearly about why he should never be allowed anywhere near Tillie."

"Good. Mention how he's lucky that you didn't go to the cops when he did what he did."

Jane sipped her tea. "Really? Do you think I should mention that? It might make him angry."

"I think you have to mention it because you could still report him, couldn't you? You could still have him charged."

"I guess so, but after all this time no one would believe it, especially now with him wanting custody. It'll look like I'm making it up to stop him." She shook her head. "I have no proof."

"Just be sure that whatever you say in the letter is calm and controlled. That way, you'll get your point across much better and he'll see you're not scared of him. If you carry on like you did just now, he'll think he's got a better chance of winning."

"*Jah*, I know you're right."

"I'm what?" He leaned over, touching his ear.

She laughed. "You're right."

He raised his eyebrows and the dimples in his cheeks made an appearance. "That's what I thought you said. Do you mind me asking where you got a name like Tillie from?"

Jane knew he was taking her mind off the altercation to calm her down. "I can't remember. I heard it somewhere. I didn't have a name for her for about three days after she was born. Everyone kept suggesting names and nothing fitted until someone said the name Tillie and I thought it just suited her."

He nodded. "It does."

She sighed. "I haven't worked so hard and gone through everything to have her taken away from me. That's not going to happen. I can't let it happen. It'd kill me."

"I'll pray for you and Tillie, and this whole situation."

"You will?"

"Of course, I will. Why wouldn't I?"

"*Denke.* That's very kind of you. And I'll ... I'll pray for you to ... find a *fraa.*"

He chuckled. "You don't have to pray for something for me just because I'm praying for something for you."

Jane looked downward. "It's not like that."

"I don't need any prayer," he said.

"That confident, are you?"

He laughed. "Not really. I'm just trying to make things easier for you and trying to be a good friend."

"A good friend would just drink his tea and be quiet."

He looked down at the mug in his hands. "It's *kaffe*."

"Whatever."

CHAPTER 13

*J*apheth and Jane sat in silence, by the warmth of the crackling fire, for several minutes and neither one of them said a word.

"You're good company," she finally said.

When he didn't speak, she looked over at him.

"Can I talk now?" he asked.

"*Jah.*"

"*Denke.* That's the nicest thing anyone's said to me for a while, especially when I haven't said a thing."

She screwed up her face. "What was nice?"

"You said I'm good company."

"You are. You made me tea and kept me calm. As well as that, you gave me good advice."

He drank the last of his coffee. "I should go. If

anyone sees me in your *haus* this late at night ..."

"Your reputation will be ruined. Mine will remain the same."

He gave a low chuckle. "I'll go back and talk to Adam and see what he wants to tell me about. He's always got things he thinks will interest me. He reads every paper and knows what everyone's up to."

"The Amish papers?"

"*Jah.* They're the only ones he reads, of course. Then I have to hear what everyone's been doing. It's boring, but he seems so happy to talk about it that I just have to sit there and listen."

"He must be enjoying having you here. Tell him I'm sorry that I don't have cupcakes for him today. I needed every one of them. The orders were all divisible by twelve."

"Do I need to add that last bit?"

"*Nee.* Well, you can if you like. He'll know. He stops by from time to time and I tell him about my cakes."

"I forgot that Adam's another friend of yours."

"*Jah*, he is. I've been meaning to ask you, why do you call him Adam?"

"I don't do it to his face. You told me you had no friends, but you've got Adam, Wendy, and me, so that's three."

"I don't think I told you I had no friends."

"I think you did."

She sniggered and made an unladylike snort from the back of her nose, which she hadn't meant.

"What's that sound for?"

"You haven't been here long enough to figure things out, so I'll tell you how it works." She shook her head. "I don't know how things work where you come from, but around here, the start is the finish. People avoid me now and they'll avoid me always. I'm unmarried and I've got a child. As far as my parents are concerned, it's irrelevant how that came about. My *mudder* says, *The facts are the facts,* which means I'm unmarried and I have a child."

"It wasn't your fault. If anything, they should be nicer to you. Anyway, even if the child had come about in the usual way, with two consenting adults, what happened to forgiveness? *Gott* forgives when we ask Him. And we should forgive, too."

"It's all about appearances. My parents think people should abstain from the 'appearance' of evil and apparently I didn't and I haven't. I don't know what they think I should do—just make Tillie disappear or something."

He shook his head. "It's not right."

"I know, but that's how things are. People are

never going to treat me the same no matter how Tillie came into this world. They can't help it. Half of them don't know what happened, but they must guess since I wasn't shunned and didn't have to confess the sin in front of the congregation."

"Yeah, they'd surely put two and two together."

"You'd think so. Anyway, I'm happy as I am doing my cupcakes and caring for Tillie, and I've got no time for a social life or for people to stop by and chatter mindlessly about nothing."

"That's a shame."

"Tell me about it. Going back to what we were talking about before, I think my parents believe I made it all up and lied to the bishop, so I can stay on in the community and avoid a shunning."

He shook his head. "It's not fair."

"It mightn't be fair, but things will never change. People are just scared. My parents are scared people will think less of them—think they were bad parents or something."

"Were they?"

"I didn't think so until this happened. They weren't there when I needed them. I'd never do that to Tillie."

He stood up and looked in her cup. "Still drinking?"

"Yeah. Leave your cup there. I'll wash it later."

"I can do it before I go."

"Leave it," she snapped.

"Yes, Ma'am."

"I'm sorry. I've been mean to you again and you've only been nice to me."

"You're under a lot of pressure."

She nodded. "I'll feel a lot better once I write that letter."

"I'll go, but you know where I am if you need anything." He made his way to the front door.

She jumped up. "Japheth!"

"*Jah?*"

"Could you do me a huge favor?"

"Sure."

"Can you post the letter tomorrow for me? Once it's on its way, I'll feel a whole lot better."

He nodded. "I'll stop by first thing and take it to the post office. I'll have to get to fixing that leak another day. Anything else?"

"*Nee, denke.*"

After he had flashed her a smile, he walked out the door. As she listened to his footsteps stomp down the porch steps, she looked back at the fire. The heat warmed her face while she sat and figured out exactly what to write in that letter.

CHAPTER 14

*J*ane woke up from the best night's sleep she'd had for some time. She looked at the clock to see that it was six thirty. Tillie was babbling to herself in her bedroom. Since she'd woken early and it didn't seem cold, Jane decided to take Tillie for a walk after breakfast.

After a quick shower, Jane pulled on her day dress and unpinned her long hair. Once she was dressed and had redone her hair, she walked into Tillie's room to see her standing up, hanging onto the railing of her crib.

"You don't have a care in the world, do you?"

Tillie reached her arms up and Jane leaned down and pulled her out of the crib. Then she changed

Tillie's diaper and dressed her for the day before they headed downstairs.

Even though Saturday was the same as any other workday, it always felt different. Things seemed slower and more relaxed somehow, and Jane was more tempted to have a rest in between times rather than continue with the frantic pace she kept up every weekday. After a breakfast of eggs and toast, she placed a blanket around Tillie before placing her in her stroller.

She pushed the stroller over the small white pebbles of the driveway to the wide road where there was plenty of room to move to one side if she happened to see a buggy or a car. Tillie was sitting upright, staring around about her.

Putting chores and work out of her mind, Jane enjoyed being out in the early morning sun and watching the soft light filter through the low branches of the trees. Everything seemed more positive and brighter when the sun was out, even though the morning air was chilly.

The walk cleared her mind and if it weren't so cold, she would've gone further. "That's it, Tillie. We'll walk again tomorrow if it's a nice day." She turned the stroller around and headed back.

When they were level with the back of Adam's *haus*, she saw Japheth hitching Adam's buggy.

Japheth looked up and saw her. "Hi, Jane."

"Hello. You're having an early start."

"Yeah. I'm helping Micah Stoltzfus repair the roof of his barn."

"That's good of you."

"On my way, I'll post that letter of yours if you have it ready."

"I do. I'll just get it for you."

Jane headed to the house, left Tillie in the stroller at the bottom of the stairs, ran inside, grabbed the letter that was already sealed and stamped, and hurried out again. She pushed Tillie back to where Japheth was and stood there watching him adjust the horse's harness.

He looked at her and smiled, then he walked over to crouch down and talk to Tillie. Tillie reached out to him and he held up his hands. "I can't touch you after I've been touching the horse. Your *Mamm* wouldn't be too happy with me." He glanced over at Jane as he stood up.

"You've got that right. Here's the letter."

"Good. I hope this is all that's needed."

"Me too. You'll be gone for the whole day?"

"Possibly. Do you need me to bring you back anything from in town?"

"*Nee denke*, and no cake either."

His eyes twinkled. "I learned that lesson."

"Wave bye-bye to Japheth, Tillie."

Tillie lifted her hand and waved. Japheth chuckled and waved back.

"Bye, Japheth," Jane said as she turned the stroller around to head back to the house.

CHAPTER 15

Several Days Later

*a*s Jane was pulling the last batch of cakes out of the oven, she heard a car. She set down the cakes, flicked off the gas, and walked the two steps to the kitchen window, surprised to see a police car coming up the shared driveway. She was even more surprised when they pulled up outside her door. Assuming they must be after directions, she opened the door. When an officer got out of the car, she walked to the edge of the porch. "Can I help you?"

A second uniformed officer got out and closed his door. They both ignored what she said and walked toward her.

The bigger one reached the porch first. "We're looking for a Jane Byler."

"That's me."

"I'm Officer Davies, and this is Officer Williams. We need you to come down to the station and answer some questions."

She looked from him to the other officer and back to the one who'd spoken. "What's this about?"

"Scott Crittenden was found dead in his apartment this morning."

She gasped and held her stomach. "Scott?"

"That's right, Ma'am. Scott Crittenden."

"Are you sure it was him?"

"Yes."

She froze and could only stare at the man in disbelief. "Are you sure? I only saw him the other day." Her knees went weak, and she collapsed onto the top step.

"We're sure. We need you to come with us. We've got some questions we'd like you to answer."

"What did he die from?"

"He was murdered."

"Murdered," she muttered quietly, trying to become accustomed to a second shock.

"Ms. Byler, we need you to come with us."

"Can you ask the questions here? I've got my baby here."

"It's quite a serious matter, Ma'am. We need to ask you a few questions regarding your relationship with him."

"I had no relationship with him. Do you think I had something to do with his murder?" When they didn't answer her, she said, "I didn't do it."

"All the same, we'll need you to come down to the station."

"I can't leave; I've got work. I work from home and I've got no one here to mind the baby and she's asleep right now."

The policemen looked at each other, Officer Williams raising his eyebrows in a quizzical manner.

She quickly added, "I'll find someone to look after the baby and then I can come as soon as I finish work at around four, or just after four. I cook for a catering company and I need to get the work done. It's my sole income. If I let my boss down, I might not get any more work and my baby and I will starve."

The officer put up his hands. "Just be there at four."

She nodded. "I will."

"Ask for Officer Davies."

"I will." She watched as they walked back to their car.

Just as they drove away, she looked up to see Japheth walking toward her.

"What was that all about?" he asked.

"Scott's dead."

He gasped. "Really?"

She nodded. "I'm worried about the letter."

His eyes grew wide. "Why?" She didn't answer, and then he asked, "Jane, what was in the letter?"

"Nothing too bad. I didn't think so at the time, anyway." She held her head. "I can't believe he's dead. He was murdered and they want to ask me questions about it. They want me to go to the station when I finish work."

"They don't think you did it, do they?"

"I'm not sure." She held her stomach. "I'll have to finish this order. Wendy can look after Tillie while I go."

"I can look after her."

She stared at him. "You told me don't know the first thing about babies."

"It can't be too hard."

"If Wendy doesn't show this afternoon, I'll stop by her *haus*, and ..."

"What if she's not home?"

THE AMISH SINGLE MOTHER

"Can I do anything to help you get the order out?"

"If you don't mind. That would be good of you."

He nodded, rolled up his sleeves, and followed her through to the kitchen.

She handed him an apron.

"Seriously?"

"You said you want to help." She pointed to liquid soap by the sink. "Wash your hands too."

When he'd washed and dried his hands, he turned around. "What do I do now?"

"While I'm mixing the frosting, you can put the cupcakes into the paper casings over there." She nodded her head to the signature casings that Miranda provided for the cupcakes, bright pink with white polka dots.

"Okay." He carefully picked up each cupcake and placed it into its casing.

"We'll be here all day if you're that slow. It's much quicker if you make rows of casings and then pop the cakes into them and do it quickly."

"Don't be too hard on me. I'm a beginner." He glanced over at her. "Don't worry; it'll be fine. You'll see."

"What if they do think I killed him?"

"They'll need proof and they don't have any because you didn't do it."

"You hear of innocent people going to jail all the time. And then there's the letter I sent him."

"Why? What was in it?" When she didn't say anything, he looked up. "Jane? What did you write in the letter?"

"I just mentioned I'd kill him if he didn't stay away from me."

His eyes opened wide and his mouth fell open. "What? You threatened him?"

She nodded. "I was desperate. I can't have her taken away. She's all I've got, and I'm all she's got. It's not as though I really meant it."

"You agreed you'd be calm, don't you remember?"

"I know. It started out that way and then I remembered how horrible he was and what he'd done. I got angry and then the letter took a different turn."

"If they find out that the two of you were heading for a legal battle over Tillie, you might be the prime suspect. I'm guessing they don't have one of those since they came here to see you."

"How is that supposed to make me feel better?"

"This is serious, Jane."

"I know it is. You don't have to tell me."

"And if they've got that letter, that'll make you look guilty."

Jane chewed on a fingernail. "What should I do?"

"You've still got his address?"

Jane nodded.

"We'll have to go to his apartment and get that letter back."

"Break in?"

"*Jah.* What choice do we have?" he asked.

"You'd do that for me?" she asked.

He frowned at her. "I'd do it for Tillie, so her mother doesn't go to jail for the rest of her life, or worse."

"It's no use. They've probably got it already and that's why they came here."

"They didn't arrest you straightaway, so that's a good sign."

"That's only because there's no law against writing an angry letter. Anyway, they would've gone right through his apartment by now looking for clues to who might've killed him. They would have the letter."

"I'll drive you to the police this afternoon."

"That's okay, I'll catch a taxi. It'll be quicker."

"I'll go with you in the taxi, then, for moral support."

She looked up at him. "You'd do that?"

"Be quiet. I'm concentrating on my job."

Jane smiled at Japheth paying her back for telling him to be quiet days before. It felt good to have someone on her side. When the contents of the letter flew through her mind, the thought instantly wiped the smile from her face.

Half an hour later, Tillie woke from her nap in the downstairs crib just as Wendy walked through the front door. After Wendy said hello to Japheth and Jane, she climbed over the railing of the dining room and picked Tillie up.

"Sorry I'm a little late. *Mamm* had me doing spring-cleaning and rug cleaning, which is the worst kind of cleaning. Is the order ready or do you need help?" She glanced at Jane's face and then looked at Japheth. "What's wrong?"

"Scott's dead," Jane said.

Wendy's mouth fell open. "*The* Scott?"

Jane nodded.

"How?"

Japheth answered, "The police said he's been murdered. They want to talk to Jane. We're taking a taxi to the station as soon as Miranda collects the order."

Wendy's gaze traveled back to Jane. "Do you want me to look after Tillie?"

"*Denke.* I was hoping you would."

"Of course, I will. Do you want us to stay here, or will I take her home? How long will you be?"

Jane glanced over at Japheth. "I'm not sure."

Japheth said, "Perhaps Wendy should take Tillie to her *haus* in case we're a long time."

"You're going with her?" Wendy asked Japheth.

He nodded. "I am."

"That's good," Wendy said as she patted Tillie on her back. "I'll make up some bottles."

"She's just started drinking from a small cup."

"I know, but she still likes her bottle and with her *Mamm* not there, she'll need comfort."

Jane didn't like to hear about her not being there. "*Denke*, Wendy. I shouldn't be too long. I hope not, anyway."

"I'm sure they just want to ask a few questions."

Jane said, "Japheth's been a big help today. We just need to box everything now." Jane glanced at the clock and saw it was fifteen minutes before Miranda would arrive.

CHAPTER 16

*A*s soon as Jane asked for Officer Davies and said who she was, she was ushered into an interview room, leaving Japheth sitting in the waiting area at the front of the station.

"We'll be recording this interview," the officer said as Jane was directed to a chair behind a table in the center of the room.

Jane nodded. "Okay."

"Would you like a lawyer or anyone to sit with you?"

"No, it's fine. I don't need a lawyer."

"It'll be a few minutes while we get the equipment set up. Would you like coffee or anything?"

"No, I'm fine."

The officer walked out of the room and Jane looked around and saw two cameras set high in the corners of the room. She fiddled nervously with her fingers on the table then moved them down to under the table in case they were watching already and she appeared too nervous.

Two officers came into the room and sat in front of her. They were the same ones who'd come to her house earlier that day.

When they sat down, Officer Davies said, "Can you state your full name for the record?"

"Jane May Byler."

"What is your relationship to Scott Crittenden?"

"We had no relationship."

"Let me ask in a different way. When did you first meet him?"

"I used to work in a restaurant and he'd come in nearly every day. He asked me out on a date nearly two years ago, and then he drugged me and raped me."

Davies moved uncomfortably in his seat. "Did you report it?"

"I didn't see any point. I didn't think anyone would believe me and his family is wealthy." She left out the part about feeling ashamed and not wanting anyone to know what had happened. If she could put it out of her mind it would be like the dreadful incident had never happened, or so she'd thought. The awful feeling of being so powerless and the feeling of being 'unclean' had never left her.

"We have a letter that you wrote to Scott. It was on his table and we found him slumped over the letter."

"Do you remember what you wrote?" Officer Williams asked.

"No. Not really. I was quite upset when I wrote it. Can I see it?"

"We have it in evidence. You can read the transcript."

Jane nodded.

The officer opened a file in front of him, pulled out a sheet of paper, and put it in front of her. She picked it up and her eyes fell to the part where she said that she would kill him if he ever came near her or Tillie again. She looked up at them. "I didn't mean I'd really kill him. It's just what people say when they're mad."

"That's what we need to find out. When was the last time you saw the deceased?"

"I don't know. A few days ago, maybe. The day I wrote the letter." She looked down at the date on the copy of the letter and read it out.

"Tell me about the conversation you had with him that last time you saw him."

"He came to my home earlier that day. When I saw him in town before then, he got the idea he was Tillie's father. I denied it and he insisted it was true, so we had an argument."

"Was he the father of your child?"

"Yes."

"But you told him he wasn't."

Jane nodded. "That's right. What rights could he have after what he did to me?"

The two officers exchanged glances.

"I didn't kill him and if you think I did you're wasting your time." Anger rose within her. "You should be out questioning someone else and trying to find the real killer."

Davies remained strangely calm. "It's convenient for you now that he's gone."

"What do you mean?"

"He's dead and he won't be bothering you anymore. It's clear from your letter you were expecting a huge fight over custody."

"Yes, it's convenient, but I didn't kill him. I'd never kill anybody."

"I've had a lot to do with the Amish people and I do find it strange for someone of your faith saying you'd kill someone. From what I know of the Amish, they're a peace-loving people—most of them, anyway."

"All I wanted was for him to stay away from me. I just wanted him to know that I was serious."

"Serious about killing him?"

"Serious that I wanted him to stay away."

"Would you submit to a polygraph test?"

"A what?"

"A lie detector test. It measures physiological indices, pulse, blood pressure, respiration—"

She pressed her lips together. "No."

"Why not, if you've got nothing to hide?"

"I don't want to do anything like that. I didn't do it and I just want to go home."

"It could look bad for you that you've refused."

Jane was scared in case the test was faulty and pointed to her being guilty. It wasn't a risk she was willing to take. "Do I have to do it?"

"No."

"Who would it look bad to?" Jane asked.

Then Williams said, "If you didn't kill him, it would be in your best interests to do a polygraph test."

She shook her head. "The truth will come out."

Officer Davies leaned forward, close enough she

could smell his body odor. "I don't think you realize the trouble you're in. If we find any evidence you were in his apartment, things will be even worse for you."

"I wasn't there. I was home all day, baking."

"He was killed during the night," Davies said.

"Oh."

"Now let's go back to when Mr. Crittenden came to your house. What did he say?"

"He said he was going to get custody of Tillie."

"Is that your daughter's name?"

"Yes, Tillie Byler."

The officer jotted it down. "Is Tillie—"

"It's just Tillie."

"And what was your response?"

"I told him I'd never allow it and he would never get Tillie when I told people what he'd done. He laughed and said no one would believe me. And I guess that's right because I didn't report it at the time."

"He made you angry. You felt threatened and afraid of losing your daughter."

Jane nodded. "Yes."

"Was it self-defense? You went to see him to talk things through and things got heated. Is that what happened?"

"No. I told you I wasn't at his house, apartment, or wherever he was staying."

After a long pause, Davies said, "Things will go a lot better for you if you tell us the truth now."

"I am telling you the truth. How much longer is this going to take?" Jane asked.

"As long as it takes you to tell us the truth."

Jane said a silent prayer to God asking Him to get her out of the mess she was in. "I didn't do it and I think that if you thought I did, you would've already arrested me by now."

"We're waiting on the lab tests to come back, as I said. This isn't done by far."

Jane rubbed her forehead, feeling a headache coming on. "I can't have been the only person to be upset with him, surely."

"It seems you are. Everyone else we've spoken with has only had good things to say about him."

"I find that hard to believe. You can't be asking the right people. He's not a nice person. Who have you been asking, his family?"

"The people you used to work with back when you claim you were raped. That's who we've asked. He was very popular among the staff and they claim you had a special relationship with him."

"That was before he did what he did. I'd thought of him as a friend, anyway."

The questions went around and around in circles like that for the next hour and then she was free to go. Jane headed to the waiting room after she signed her statement. She found Japheth in the waiting area.

He leaped to his feet as soon as he saw her. "How did it go?"

"Dreadful."

He clasped both her hands. "You're shaking. What did they say?"

She looked around about her, and whispered, "They think I did it."

"Surely they don't."

"They just don't have enough evidence yet to arrest me."

His eyes widened. "Is that what they said?"

Jane nodded.

Just as they were leaving the waiting room, a small woman with heavily lacquered tall black hair stepped in front of her. "Are you Jane Byler?"

She was almost scared to say yes from the look of the woman. "I am."

"Where's my granddaughter?"

"Who are you?"

"I'm Scott's mother."

Jane looked down. "I'm sorry about your son."

Tears streamed down the woman's face. "My granddaughter?"

"She's not here."

"You can't keep her away from us. You're a dreadful, dreadful woman. I'm taking you to court."

Jane opened her mouth to speak, but Japheth took a firm hold of her arm and started walking, taking her along with him. "Don't say a thing, Jane."

All she could do was trust Japheth and listen to him because she was too upset and worked up to think clearly.

"You made up the story about my son and you'll be sorry. He told me what really happened. You won't get away with it," the woman called after her.

Jane freed herself from Japheth's grasp and turned around. "When did he tell you?"

"Two days ago. I know about girls like you who go after men with money. You deliberately got pregnant to latch on to him. You probably killed him too."

Jane turned back, broke out of Japheth's grasp, and said to the woman, "I don't want any—"

Japheth pulled on her arm, moving her away again. As soon as they were outside the police station, he hailed a passing taxi and guided her into the back seat before he climbed in after her.

When he barked out his address to the driver, Jane put both hands over her face and sobbed.

Japheth moved closer and put his arm around her. "It'll work out."

"I'm in a dreadful nightmare. I thought things were bad enough and now they just got worse, much worse. They didn't believe anything I said."

hen they pulled up near the house, Wendy walked over from her house, holding Tillie and the diaper bag.

"What happened?" Wendy asked.

"It's a long story."

"I'll make us tea," Wendy said after she handed Tillie to her mother.

Tillie put her arms around her mother's neck and put her head on her shoulder.

Wendy patted Tillie on her back. "She missed you."

Jane turned to Japheth, and called out, "Are you coming inside?"

"*Jah.*"

When they were all seated in the living room with Tillie on Jane's lap, Japheth said he was going to ask around to see if anyone knew of a lawyer and mentioned Adam might know one.

"How would Adam know of a lawyer, Japheth?" Wendy asked.

"He's been living in this area long enough. He knows everyone. He'll know someone who knows a good lawyer, someone to do with family law," Japheth said.

Wendy nodded. "That's what we need, a family law specialist."

Jane didn't need more worries. "I can't believe he's dead. It's like I'm in a bad dream. I mean, he was Tillie's father, not that I wanted her to have anything to do with him. It doesn't seem real somehow."

"It's a shock," Japheth said in a sympathetic tone.

After she gave a huge sigh, Jane said, "I can't get a lawyer. I've got no money. I'll have to represent myself at court."

Japheth shook his head. "That would be a dreadful idea."

"I've got no choice. People can represent themselves, defend themselves or whatever the correct terminology is."

Frowning at her, Japheth said, "You're too fiery, and hot tempered. You'd lose your cool."

Jane looked at him, knowing what he said was true.

"Don't worry. I'll find a cheap lawyer," Japheth said.

"*Kaffe*, Japheth?" Wendy asked.

"*Nee denke.*"

"He or she might not be any good if they're cheap," Jane said in response to his earlier comment.

Wendy filled the kettle with water, while Japheth said, "Trust me, I'll find one. Perhaps they could set up some sort of payment plan."

"You think so?" Jane asked.

He nodded. "Leave it with me."

"*Denke*, Japheth. I don't know what I would've done if you weren't here."

"Just relax and don't think the worst all the time."

"It's pretty hard to stop fearful thoughts flashing through my mind."

"Do your best," he said.

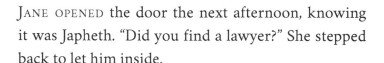

JANE OPENED the door the next afternoon, knowing it was Japheth. "Did you find a lawyer?" She stepped back to let him inside.

He took a giant step into the house. "I found someone who's supposed to be very good."

"Supposed to be?"

"He is very good. Trust me."

He kept telling her to trust him, but trusting people wasn't easy. Japheth had been good to her so far and had not given her one reason not to trust him. He seemed just as nice as his grandfather.

"His name is Philip Primrose-Peabody."

Giggles rang out from the kitchen. A smile slowly crept over Japheth's face. "It doesn't matter what his name is, Wendy."

"I'm sorry," Wendy called out from the kitchen.

Jane said, "I don't care what his name is as long as he can get the job done."

"Exactly. We've got an appointment to see him tomorrow at four thirty."

"We?"

His lips tilted upward.

"You're coming with me?"

"If you want me to."

"Yes. I'd like you to come with me. I'm glad we could get in to see him so soon." She put a hand to her heart. "I probably need two lawyers, one that does criminal law and one for family law."

"Relax. You haven't been arrested for anything to

do with Scott's murder. Don't go thinking too far ahead. I thought four thirty would be a good time because that gives us enough time to get the delivery collected and get into town. And I can help you tomorrow. You'll just need to show me what to do."

"Hey, can I get some help in here?" the voice from the kitchen asked.

"Coming." Jane spun around and headed to the kitchen with Japheth not far behind her.

"What can I do?" Japheth asked.

"Just watch what we do for now," Wendy said.

He slouched against the wall with his arms across his chest. "I'm a fast learner," he said.

"There'll be plenty for you to do tomorrow," Jane said.

THE NEXT MORNING, Jane stood at the window, getting the milk ready for Tillie's morning drink. She'd just started several slices of bread toasting, too. When she looked up at Adam's house through the window, she saw Japheth strolling over to her house with a mug in his hand.

"He's early," she said to Tillie who was sitting in her high chair up at the table.

"Don't move a muscle," she said to Tillie as she raced to open the front door. "Come in," she yelled to Japheth and then she walked back to the kitchen. She immediately checked the bread under the grill. The last thing she needed was another accident with burned food.

He walked into the kitchen. "Hello there."

"Hello."

"You didn't exactly tell me what time to come. I know you start early, so I wasn't sure."

She glanced over at him. "Have a seat."

He sat down, reached forward, and tickled Tillie under her chin, which made her laugh. "Do you want me to come back a little later?"

"*Nee*, that's fine. I'll start just as soon as we finish breakfast. You can stay."

She placed small strips of toast in front of Tillie who preferred to feed herself with things she could hold in her hand. Even at this age, she was showing an independent streak.

"I can't wait to get started."

Jane giggled. "I'm glad you're enthusiastic."

"I am. I've never made cookies before. I mean cupcakes. I just don't know what my friends would say about it."

"What? A man in the kitchen? You were telling

me the other day that it wasn't so surprising. Adam has to cook for himself and so does any man who's not married. Otherwise, they'd starve."

"Not if they bought take-out."

Jane's eyebrows rose. "That could end up expensive."

"True."

"*Denke* for helping me today. With you and Wendy around the house so much, I don't feel so alone."

"I'm glad I'm being of some help to someone on my short stay here. I still haven't gotten to that roof leak yet. I've got that next on the list. Adam's kept me busy with a few things over there."

Jane nodded, wondering just how long that stay would be if he called it a short stay. He'd said his mother wanted him to look for a wife while he was there but was that what he wanted?

When they had finished their breakfast, Tillie was placed in the playpen while Jane proceeded to show Japheth how to cream the butter and the sugar with the gas-powered mixer.

"Doesn't Tillie ever get bored in there by herself?"

"She's not by herself; she can see us. And there are plenty of things in there to keep her occupied and I play with her every chance I get between batches."

He nodded. Did he think she wasn't being attentive enough to Tillie? Everything was a balance, a juggling act—the balance that every working mother had to strike. Something had to give and sometimes it was everything that had to give a little, in order to get everything accomplished. There was no use explaining that to someone like Japheth, who had only ever had himself to worry about.

Once they had the first batch in the oven, it was on to spooning the cake-batter mixture into the next lot of trays.

"Just as well you've got so many trays."

"It saves time. I'm all about saving time."

She studied the careful concentration on his face as he spooned just the right amount of batter into each section. The silence was a welcome change and she was glad he wasn't giving her a lecture about a larger oven, or telling her how to run her life.

"I am saving up for a bigger oven," Jane mentioned out of the blue.

"I know, you told me. Why didn't you just ask Adam to put in a big one for you?"

Jane gasped. "I couldn't do that."

"Why not?"

"I just couldn't. He's already been so good to me."

"It wouldn't make any difference to him. He's got a lot of money, and I can tell he's really pleased how you're making a life for yourself and Tillie."

"But still, it's not my money. And I told you, he lets me stay here for practically nothing."

"He could get you a larger oven and then you could pay a little extra in rent. You wouldn't be paying it off because it wouldn't be yours, it would belong to the house, but you would have use of it. Adam could perhaps cover his costs with just a little more rent."

"I knew you were thinking of something. You weren't concentrating on the cakes at all, were you?"

He laughed. "You got me."

"It's a solution, but it's not a solution that I'm going to approach Adam about. I just couldn't." She picked up the wooden spoon and waved it at him. "And you're not going to mention it either."

"I won't, if you don't want me to."

"I don't."

Once the first lot of cakes was out of the oven and the second lot was in, Tillie started to wail. "That signals her nap time. She has a sleep in the morning and one in the afternoon."

"And you put her upstairs or in the crib in there?"

He nodded toward the old dining room, which was now the playroom.

"Either one." She climbed over the railing. "I'll change her diaper and give her a bottle, and she might go to sleep upstairs. Watch the cakes for me and take them out when the buzzer chimes?"

"Sure. I'm glad to see you're using a timer now."

She rolled her eyes and remained silent while she took Tillie out of the playroom.

When Tillie was in her crib, Jane came downstairs. Japheth had the second lot out of the oven and he already had another lot ready to go in.

"I'm impressed," Jane said, looking at the work he'd done.

"*Denke.* That means a lot coming from you."

She giggled. "You can have a break now if you wish."

"A lunch break?"

"*Jah.*"

"Okay, I guess I better go and say hello to old Adam."

"Just don't let him hear you call him that."

"I won't. I'll be back as soon as I have something to eat."

Jane ate a quick lunch from leftovers and was taking the third lot of cakes out of the oven when

Wendy arrived at the same time as Japheth came back from his break.

"Where's Tillie?" Wendy asked.

At that same moment, Tillie cried.

"She must've heard your voice," Jane said.

A smile spread across Wendy's face. "I'll go get her."

Japheth placed his hands on his hips. "What do I do now?"

"We mix up the frosting. The earlier ones can be frosted now, but the other ones have to cool awhile. Actually, there's nothing much for you to do now."

"There must be something for me to do around here. I could get started on the roof."

Jane shook her head. "No, don't. I'm so nervous about going to the lawyer this afternoon that I can't think about anything else. I just want to focus on the cupcakes and then have a clear mind for the appointment this afternoon."

"Fair enough. Do you mind if I hang around and watch how you create the masterpieces?"

"You're welcome to stay and watch."

A smile beamed across his face.

AFTER MIRANDA HAD LEFT with the order, and

Wendy had taken Tillie to her house, Japheth called for a taxi.

Japheth and Jane waited on her porch for their ride.

"*Denke* for coming with me. I wouldn't have liked to go alone."

"I'm happy to be there if it makes you feel better."

They continued to wait and it struck Jane as odd that for such an important occasion as this, her family was nowhere to be seen. A man, who'd been a stranger to her just days ago, he was the one who would sit by her side at the lawyer's. She bounded to her feet when the taxi appeared.

CHAPTER 18

*A*s they sat in the back seat of the taxi, Japheth glanced over at her. "Nervous?"

"Very nervous." She swallowed hard and struggled to breathe.

"We must trust that everything will work out well."

She rubbed her face with both hands. Life could've been worse. Money was coming in, she had a place to live, and there were some people in the community who supported her. Her situation could've been worse.

When Jane and Japheth stepped out of the taxi, they saw from the names on the office window that Primrose-Peabody worked with at least four other lawyers. Their office was in a prime position, being directly opposite the courthouse. Jane added up everything in her mind. Going by the name of *Peabody-Primrose, Morgan, Stanford, and McDonald,* Peabody-Primrose was a partner and judging by the position of the office, none of this would come cheap.

Just as well they'd offered a payment plan. Whatever it cost her was going to be worth it because there was no price on Tillie's future, and she had to keep her away from the Crittenden family. Scott had clearly lied to his family and now they were out to ruin her life.

Japheth reached high over Jane's head to push the door of the office open for her to walk through first. In front of her was a large marble-like reception area.

Jane cleared her throat when the well-groomed secretary looked up. "We're here to see Mr. Primrose-Peabody."

She smiled and glanced at the computer screen beside her. "Jane Byler?"

"Yes."

"He won't be a moment. Would you like to take a seat?" She gestured to two couches off to the side.

Jane's fingernails found their way to her mouth while they waited.

"Don't be worried. This is just a preventative

measure. They haven't even seen a lawyer as far as we know."

"I know."

Jane was deliberately keeping her mind occupied by counting the squares on the wallpaper when a small balding man appeared in the hallway. "Jane Byler?"

"Yes."

"Come through." Jane stood up and then turned around to see Japheth was still seated. "Please come in with me. I mightn't remember everything he says."

"Sure." Japheth bounded to his feet.

A few steps further down the hall and they were in Primrose-Peabody's office. He closed the door behind them. "Have a seat."

There were two office chairs in front of a desk and when Jane sat down, she looked around the office to see sporting memorabilia on the walls. Her attention was particularly taken with a boxing glove behind a gold frame.

As soon as the lawyer was seated, he began, "From what I understand, you are a single parent and someone who claims he is the father of your child has stepped forward and is threatening to take the child away from you."

"That's right."

The lawyer asked her the names of the individuals concerned, and after he'd jotted them down, he looked back up at her. "I know the Crittendens quite well."

Jane gasped. "They're not clients of yours, are they?"

His thin lips curled upward. "If they were, I wouldn't be speaking with you. I know the law firm and the lawyers they use. We should be able to keep this out of the courts and get it resolved fairly quickly." He made some notes again and looked up at Jane. "Scott Crittenden is the father, you say?"

"Yes, but only because he raped me."

He blinked a couple of times. "Did he ever admit to that?"

"No. He denied it."

"Of course he would've." He put his pen down and leaned back in his chair. "I take it you never made a police report?"

Jane shook her head. "No. I didn't. And I denied it to Scott when he asked me if the child was his. Still, he seemed convinced that she was."

"I guess that changes things quite a bit, does it?" Japheth asked.

"It could get messy. Are you willing to give the family any visitation?"

"Absolutely not!" Anger rose within Jane and she was calmed by Japheth softly placing his fingertips on her arm. "I don't want them anywhere near her. He was a violent and horrible person, and from what I've seen of his mother she's just the same."

"Just to be clear, you didn't file a report after the rape took place?"

"No."

"And why is that?" the lawyer asked.

"He drugged me and I didn't think anyone would believe me. I can remember glimpses of it and I remember fading in and out of consciousness. I didn't have any bruises on me or any signs of violence, because the drug made me unable to fight his assault, so I didn't think anyone would believe me."

"It would've been better if you'd filed a complaint or made some attempt to have him charged. But we can't do anything about that now."

"I didn't know. And of course I didn't know I had become pregnant from the rape until later."

He leaned forward and picked up his pen.

"What happens now?" Japheth asked.

"I'll get in touch with their lawyers and see if we can resolve this thing quickly, and keep it out of court."

Jane clasped her hands tightly in her lap. "But what does that mean? There's no compromise here. I don't want them to see her at all."

"Their first step would likely be to prove paternity, which means they'd place an order to have your child DNA tested. That would be the first step. I'll make a call and see what their intentions are and how far they're willing to go with all this."

Jane nodded. "That would be good. Thank you."

His thin lips turned upward at the corners. "Until then, Ms. Byler, try not to worry."

Japheth said, "That's easier said than done. Jane's been through a lot already and this is something she doesn't need."

Jane blinked back tears. "I thought he moved to New York and I thought I'd never have to see him again."

Japheth placed a hand on her shoulder.

"Is there any way I can contact you by phone?" the lawyer asked with pen poised.

Shaking her head, she said, "No, I don't have a phone, but I could call you tomorrow afternoon."

"I have a phone where I'm staying. I can give you that number. I'm staying next door to Jane."

"And your name?"

"Japheth Fisher."

"And you're a relative of Jane's?"

" A friend." Japheth gave him the number of the phone in his grandfather's barn.

"Very good. I'll call you as soon as I know anything and also send you a letter, so you'll have everything in writing. I don't suppose either of you have email?"

They both shook their heads.

"And what about money? What do I owe you for today?" Jane asked.

"We'll worry about all that later. It's something I can't tell you until I know where we stand with the Crittenden family. These kinds of cases can vary greatly." He stood up.

Japheth stood as well. "Thank you."

Jane was the last to get to her feet. It felt awful being so helpless and not being able to do anything herself. Leaving it in someone else's hands was an odd feeling.

"Come on, Jane," Japheth whispered.

When they were back outside, Jane took several deep breaths to calm herself. "We're taking on the whole family and they're wealthy and they have lawyers. He said he knows the lawyers they use. That means they must sue people all the time, and they've got more than one lawyer."

"Not necessarily. Sometimes people in business use lawyers for all kinds of things." He rested his hand gently on her shoulder. "Let's go somewhere for a drink before we go home."

"I don't drink."

"Tea, coffee, ice cream? Let's just go somewhere before I take you home again."

She slowly nodded. "I'd like that."

CHAPTER 19

*J*apheth nodded his head toward a café up the road. "That must be where people go before and after they go to court."

"Let's go there, then." She started walking and he followed.

Once they were inside the small café, they squeezed into a booth and Japheth passed the menu over to her. "My treat."

"I do have money, you know. You don't have to pay for everything."

"That's what men do. Men look after women."

She managed a smile as she picked up the menu. She hadn't had anyone look after her for a long time. Not only did he make her feel calm, he also made her feel protected.

"I think I'll have a chocolate shake."

"Is that all?"

She touched her stomach. "I couldn't eat a thing."

He shook his head. "That's what you always say. Why don't you have a sandwich or something?"

"I truly couldn't eat anything. Don't let me stop you having something."

"No one could stop that." He ordered a serve of waffles and kept her company by also having a shake. Once the waitress left, he said, "Don't feel threatened, like it's just you against the whole Crittenden family. You've got *Gott* on your side."

"*Gott?*"

"*Jah*, remember Him?"

Jane managed to smile. "I'm sorry, I thought you said something else."

"If we have *Gott*, nothing can come in our way. You've got Him fighting your battles, so don't worry."

"I'm sorry, but sometimes I think horrible things. Like where was *Gott* when I was attacked? Why didn't He stop it?"

"Why didn't He?"

She nodded.

"You should know why every time you look into your little girl's face."

Jane exhaled a deep breath. "That's true. I wouldn't have Tillie. But couldn't I have had Tillie after I was married, so she could've had a *vadder* and proper *familye*? And maybe my parents as proper grandparents?"

"I know what you mean. I really don't have the answers and I don't think anyone does. Sometimes we just have to take the good with the bad and stop trying to find reasons why the bad things happen."

"Was He punishing me?"

"I don't believe so. It's part of being human and living on this earth. Bad things happen to good people sometimes." He shrugged his shoulders. "Many people believe *Gott* tests his children, but sometimes really horrible things happen and I don't think He has anything to do with it."

Jane sucked on her straw. "I'll never know."

"Don't let what happened come between you and *Gott*."

"I did for a long time, wondering if He had allowed it to happen. I came back to the community after it happened and I thought it might have been *Gott's* way of bringing me back. But, if He's the Almighty, He could've done that in some other way."

"Who knows? I firmly believe He wants us to

trust and keep trusting because he knows the end from the beginning."

Jane rubbed her neck and then sudden tears flowed down her face. Japheth slid out from his seat and moved to sit next to her. He put his arm around her shoulders and held her tight. "I wish I could make it all better for you and take away the horrible thing that happened."

She continued to sob and he passed her a paper napkin and she wiped her eyes. "I'm sorry. I'm a mess."

"That's understandable. Who wouldn't be? You've been through so much, but some of it might be coming to an end soon."

"I thought it was over when he died. I thought he'd be out of my life for good."

WHEN THEY STEPPED out of the taxi at Jane's house, Japheth said, "Are you okay?"

She shook her head. "When I get upset like this, I often get a migraine."

"Have you got one now?"

She put a hand to her head. "I can feel one coming on."

"Do you take anything for them?"

"Nothing works. Painkillers don't work and I haven't found anything that does except a cold wash-cloth and just sleeping it off."

"I'll come with you to Wendy's to get Tillie. Maybe you should stay at my *haus* tonight, or at Wendy's?"

"I'll be okay."

"What if you're so sick you can't look after Tillie?"

"It'll be okay. I'll have Sally, Wendy's mother, check on me first thing in the morning."

"Will you?"

"I will. I'll be all right. I've gotten used to living by myself. You go fix Adam some dinner."

"Are you sure?"

She nodded. "I'm quite sure."

"I'll stop by to check on you tomorrow."

"Okay. *Denke* for everything you've done, Japheth."

"I haven't done much at all."

"You have. You've been there to keep me calm and you found the lawyer. He seems to know what he's doing. I don't know what I would've done without you."

"It's nothing. Now go and fetch Tillie."

She gave him a big smile and then they each turned and went their separate ways.

Jane knew the signs of the migraines that plagued her every few weeks. There was the feeling of not being in her body, the sparkles at the edges of her vision, and the nausea that would soon be swirling in her stomach.

She knocked on the door of Wendy's home and Wendy's mother, Sally, opened it.

"We were just talking about you." She stepped back to let Jane through the door.

"Were you?"

"We were just saying we thought you'd be coming home soon."

She looked over to the living room and saw Tillie asleep on the couch with Wendy sitting beside her. "She's asleep?"

"Tillie was upset and was asking for you and she's only just fallen asleep."

"She was asking for me?"

"She was saying, 'Mamma, Mamma.'"

Jane smiled.

"Jane, would you stay for dinner? We've got plenty."

The thought of not having to cook dinner pleased Jane immensely. "I'd like that, *denke*."

After Wendy had gotten up from the couch, she searched Jane's face. "How did things go?"

"*Jah*, Wendy told me where you were. Did things go okay?" Sally asked.

"I think everything went okay, but it's put me under so much stress that I fear I might be having another migraine coming on."

Sally turned to Wendy. "Wendy, would you stay at Jane's tonight?"

"You want me to stay with you, Jane?"

Jane could only nod. These people had become like a family and she didn't know what she would've done without them. Her migraines were debilitating and it would've been so hard to look after Tillie with one of her full-blown migraines. "*Denke*, Wendy."

"And don't worry about the cupcakes; I can cook them myself tomorrow. Don't worry," Wendy said.

"I should be okay. I might not get a headache."

"I can do it all myself if you do."

"What about the piping?" Jane asked.

Wendy smiled. "I've been practicing."

"Have you?"

"*Jah.* I figured out it's all in the wrist motion. I

only had problems with finishing the piping and now I've perfected that with a flick of my wrist."

"I suppose it *is* all in the wrist. I never really thought about it." Jane's gaze traveled to Tillie's small face, as she lay asleep on the couch. She was a perfectly wonderful child, which was amazing considering who her father was.

CHAPTER 20

*J*ane went to sleep that night with everything she would need for the impending migraine. On her nightstand were painkillers, even though she was certain they didn't do much good, a large glass of water, and a washcloth on a plate.

She woke in the middle of the night with a migraine and she summoned all her strength to sit up and take the painkillers. After she had swallowed the pills with a mouthful of water, she poured water on the washcloth and then lay back down, spreading the wet cloth on her forehead. There wasn't much of a chance she'd get any sleep that night. The best defense, she'd learned, was to let her body go and relax. Holding tension in her body only made things worse.

153

She deliberately relaxed her shoulders, neck, and facial muscles while visualizing lying beside a beautiful waterfall and crystal-clear flowing stream.

The next time she came awake, sunlight was streaming into the room from the open curtains in her bedroom.

Then she heard a whisper.

"Jane, how are you feeling?"

She looked around to see Wendy. "Not good. I'm so glad you stayed over."

"Can I get you anything?"

"Ice. Can you put some in my washcloth?"

"*Jah*." She stepped forward and took it from her.

"How's Tillie?"

"She's fine. We've had breakfast and she's gone back to sleep. I've got the first of the cakes in the oven. Don't worry about a thing; I can handle it all. You just close your eyes and I'll get ice inside the cloth and put it on your forehead."

Having no strength to answer, Jane closed her eyes. Minutes later, she felt an icy-cold wet washcloth being applied to her forehead and then she heard Wendy tiptoe away.

When Jane opened her eyes some time later, she turned to see salty crackers on her nightstand. She sat up and managed to munch on one. Worried about Tillie and the cupcakes, she summoned some energy and pulled on her dressing gown in readiness to walk downstairs. When she heard a male voice coming from downstairs, she sat back down on her bed.

Japheth was in the house. He said he'd come and help out if she was ill. She wasn't ready to see anyone looking like the fright that she was, but she had to check on things. If she lost Miranda's business, it would be hard to find someone else to buy so many cupcakes. She exchanged the dressing gown and her nightgown for a dress, and then leaned over, and grabbed her prayer *kapp* and placed it on her head, pushing her hair underneath. Then she made her way to the kitchen.

Japheth was packaging the cupcakes when she walked into the kitchen. "How are you feeling?"

"Better."

"Jane, you look dreadful. You should go back to bed."

"Where's Tillie?"

"She's just gone down for a nap."

"Thanks for helping, Japheth."

"It's been fun."

Jane managed a smile, figuring he wouldn't think that after he'd done twenty thousand of them. The frosting on the cakes wasn't executed quite as well as she could do it, but it was a satisfactory effort. "You've improved, Wendy."

"I told you I've been practicing."

She glanced up at Japheth, who was frowning at her. "*Denke* to both of you."

"I'm glad you're a little better," Japheth said.

He and Wendy both looked back at Jane.

"Do you think you can eat something, Jane?" Wendy asked.

"Maybe. Maybe a little bit of something. I had those crackers. Could you make me a sandwich?"

"Sure."

Japheth put the last cupcake into the box. "All done." He glanced at the clock on the wall. "All done with fifteen minutes to spare."

"That's *wunderbaar*."

He sat down next to Jane. "Have you been to the doctor about your headaches?"

"I've been to more than one. I've tried a few different medications and nothing works for me. There's something preventative that I can take every day, but I don't like to do that."

"What do you want on your sandwich, Jane?"

"Just whatever is there. Cheese will do. Would you like one too, Japheth?"

"Nee denke."

When they heard a car pull up, Japheth looked out the window. "She's early." He gathered the boxes, carefully placing one on top of the other, and headed out the door.

CHAPTER 21

Several Days Later

Japheth climbed down from the ladder and headed inside Jane's house. "That's the roof fixed."

"Really? You fixed it?" It was early evening and Jane was in the middle of peeling vegetables for dinner.

"Just the roof. I still have to fix the ceiling and I'll need to get the proper equipment and materials for that. I'm going to that barn raising tomorrow and I'll find out from one of the men where's the best place to get the plasterboard for the ceiling."

"Would that be expensive?"

"It won't be much at all and you won't be paying for it."

"But I've been living here and I've probably made it worse since I didn't tell Adam when it first happened."

"Don't worry about it. It won't cost much, just a few cents."

"*Denke.* It's nice of you to repair it."

"I'm only doing it because it's Adam's house." He smirked at her and she looked away.

Jane knew he liked her. "I didn't know you were going to the barn raising tomorrow."

He sat down at the table with her. "You're not going?"

"How can I? Who would make the cupcakes? The cupcake fairy?"

He raised his hands. "It was just a question. Don't get agitated."

Even though he liked her, he would probably rather a woman who got involved more with things —the type of woman who would get involved with helping with the food for the barn raising. "I could've baked cupcakes for the workers. I should've done that."

He laughed. "Cupcakes are too fancy for them. Don't worry about it."

"Do you think so?"

He nodded. "I won't leave the ceiling too long. I'll have it patched up in a few days. At least the rain will stay out now." He clapped his hands together. "Now, what other jobs do you have for me?"

"Nothing."

"I know there's something. I'm sure you mentioned the other day that there was something else that needed doing. Perhaps quite a few things?"

"There's a window upstairs in the spare room that doesn't close properly. The wind whistles through. I've put a towel there to keep out the cold."

"That's not good."

"I know."

"How big is the gap?"

"Not much at all. It's only when it's really cold in wintertime that I feel it."

"I'll have a quick look."

Jane placed her peeling knife on the counter. "I'll show you."

He stood in front of the window and tried unsuccessfully to open it and then he tried to close it. "It's stuck."

"I know. That's what I said."

"I didn't realize that you meant it wouldn't go up, either. It's not as if I didn't believe you."

"Good."

He looked around and saw a chair, and then pulled it over to the window. He stood on the chair, and then he put all his weight behind the window frame and forced it closed. "There, that solves that problem for now. I'm no expert on windows. I'm sure there'll be someone at the barn raising who can tell me how to fix it properly." He got down from the chair and put it back where it had been. Looking at Jane, he asked, "What else?"

"Nothing. There's nothing else. Not that I can think of at the moment."

"Okay, then I should get back to old Adam."

≈

THE NEXT DAY when Miranda had been and gone, Jane was left alone to think about Japheth. He seemed too good to be true. Maybe there was something about him she didn't know. Something that was not so good if his mother had wanted him to come to this community to find a wife.

She'd been meaning to talk to Adam, hoping to find out whether Japheth had mentioned anything about a new and bigger oven. That would be embarrassing and she hoped that Japheth had left that subject well and truly alone.

"Tillie, we're going to visit Adam." She picked Tillie up out of the highchair and headed to Adam's house. She'd get him talking and hopefully find out a few things.

She knocked on Adam's door, hoping he would be awake. Since he opened the door pretty quickly, she didn't think he'd been asleep.

His large frame filled the doorway as he stared at them both. "What a delightful surprise. Are you here to see me or Japheth? Because he's not here."

Jane gave an embarrassed giggle. "We're here to see you. You haven't been to the *haus* lately and we thought we'd pay you a visit."

"*Gut.* Come inside." He led her through to the kitchen and turned around. "I should take you to the living room, not the kitchen.

"Here's fine."

"*Jah?*"

She nodded and sat down with Tillie on her lap.

When Adam sat, he made funny faces at Tillie to make her laugh. She giggled like Jane had never heard her laugh before.

Adam chuckled. "It works better when she hasn't seen me for a while."

"It seems so. Where's Japheth?"

"He's at the barn raising. Didn't he tell you?"

"He might have."

"You've been seeing a bit of him."

"He's been such a huge help to me. I don't know if he told you anything that's been going on?"

"He did. He said Tillie's father … Well, he told me about what happened with him being murdered. I'm very sorry to hear that."

"Japheth has been very supportive to me. He's a really nice man." This was Adam's opportunity to say something if he knew something to the contrary.

"Wouldn't you expect that from my *grosskin*?" Adam chuckled.

Jane smiled and nodded, wondering how else she could find out more about Japheth without asking outright. "Did you have much to do with him when he was growing up?"

"*Jah*, a fair amount. They lived here before they moved away."

"So, he's as nice as he seems?" It was hardly subtle, but she couldn't think of any other way to ask the question since Adam wasn't coming forward with any information of his own.

He stared at Jane. "He is. How about a cup of hot tea?"

"*Denke*, Adam. Would you like to hold Tillie while I make it?"

He chuckled. "Okay."

Jane stood up and passed Tillie over. Adam bounced her up and down on his knee and Tillie squealed with delight.

Jane passed the next hour or so chatting with Adam and was satisfied that there was nothing dark about Japheth. Or if there was, Adam knew nothing.

IT WAS EARLY the next day when she saw Japheth again. He was walking purposefully to the house and she hoped he wasn't upset she'd been talking about him to Adam. With Tillie on one hip, she opened the front door with her free hand.

"I got a call from Primrose-Peabody. He's coming here just after four. He wanted to tell you something in person."

"*Ach nee*. I hope it's not bad news."

"He didn't say. It was actually his secretary who called. I can't be here because I told someone I'd meet him at the hardware store to buy the plaster-board for the ceiling repair. He's showing me exactly what to get. Unless I get in touch with him and change the time."

"*Nee*, you go as planned. Don't change the time. I'll be able to handle it, no matter whether it's good news or bad."

"It's probably good news."

"I hope so. *Denke* for letting me know. Do you want to come in?"

"*Nee*, I was in the middle of cooking breakfast for Adam when the call came. I'll go back and finish it." Japheth pulled a face. "Then he wants to talk with me."

Jane hoped Adam wouldn't say she'd been over there asking questions about him. "Okay. I'll let you know what it's about when you get home this evening."

"I'll come here as soon as I get back."

Jane nodded, and then Japheth turned and walked away.

Throughout the day, Jane did her best to concentrate on the cupcakes, but all she could do was worry about what the lawyer might have to say.

When a car pulled up outside her house just as Miranda drove away with the order, she ran to the door and opened it. Mr. Primrose-Peabody was getting out of his car. She studied his face and couldn't tell whether he had good news or bad.

"What is it?" she asked as she ran to him.

"How about we go inside and I'll tell you when we're sitting down."

"Yes, of course. I'm sorry, I'm forgetting my manners."

She showed him into the living room and when they were seated, he said, "I've got something to tell you that you'll be pleased about."

"What is it?"

"The Crittendens are not proceeding with the custody case."

A load lifted off her shoulders and she exhaled heavily. "That's good. Can they still try something else?"

"I don't think they'd be likely to do anything. I heard that a friend of Scott Crittenden came forward and told the Crittendens exactly what happened regarding you. He produced a text that showed Scott boasting about what he did to you. And after that, Scott and his friend parted ways, but his friend kept the text. When he heard of Scott's death and the rumors that his parents were trying to take your baby, he came forward."

"I'm so pleased. That must've been Bonnie." She

hadn't seen Bonnie since the incident. He could've been the one who'd had the falling out with Scott.

"I don't think they'll be bothering you again. It'll be up to you whether your child has a relationship with them."

"No. Definitely not. They're not nice people."

"That's up to you."

"Thank you for coming all this way to tell me."

"It's not that far. It was on my way home and you don't have a phone. I wanted to tell you in person." He looked around him.

She pushed herself back into the couch. "I can't believe it's all over. Well, mostly over. Do you know if they found out who killed him yet?"

"I haven't heard." He rose to his feet. "I'll leave you to it."

Jumping to her feet with renewed energy, she inquired, "How much do I owe you for everything?"

"That's all been taken care of."

"What do you mean?"

"Someone has stepped forward on your behalf to take care of the financial side of things."

She put a hand to her throat and tried to figure out who it would be. "The Crittendens?"

He chuckled. "No."

She knew it wasn't her parents and the only

person she could think of was her new friend. "Japheth Fisher?"

"I believe the person didn't want to be named." He gave a slight raise of his eyebrows before he walked toward the door.

Managing to get there first, she opened the door for him. Standing in a daze, she watched the lawyer walk down the porch steps and get into his car.

When he drove away, she marched over to Adam's house and knocked on the door, hoping Japheth was home. Japheth opened the door and she told him the good news.

"Scott's family is dropping things. They found out the truth from a former friend of Scott's, and I don't have to worry about anything anymore." That wasn't quite true; she knew she wasn't in the clear over Scott's murder.

He stepped outside with her. "That's *wunderbaar.*"

"Japheth, did you pay the lawyer?"

His lips twitched. "I had some savings. Don't make a big deal out of it."

She threw her arms around his neck and kissed him on his cheek.

He pulled her arms away and placed them down by her sides. "Adam might see."

"Well, tell him how truly *wunderbaar* you are."

"He already knows that."

Jane giggled. "I'll pay you back every cent."

"*Nee*, you will not! Let's not get into an argument about that because I'll win. I'm really happy for you that everything turned out well, Jane."

He seemed strangely distant. "You don't seem very happy."

"Adam says he's okay and I should go home, back to my job. He's politely kicking me out."

Jane stepped back. "You're leaving?"

He nodded. "Yeah. I'm not sure when."

"You'll be at the meeting on Sunday, won't you?"

"What's today?"

"Friday. And the meeting's on this Sunday."

"*Jah.* I will. I'll let you know way ahead of time before I go. We'll have to celebrate me leaving."

Jane pouted. "It's not a celebration."

"Where's Tillie?"

"She's fast asleep." She glanced back at her house. "I better get back home."

"I'll stop by tomorrow and fix that ceiling if that's okay."

"Of course. I'll be there all day. I'm not going anywhere. They still don't know who killed Scott."

"Don't worry. I'm sure if they thought it was you, they would've arrested you by now."

"I know, but it's hanging over my head because of the letter and everything. Can't you stay until that's sorted?"

He looked down at the ground. "Some murder cases are never solved." When he looked back at her, he said, "Cheer up. It's not as though I'm leaving tomorrow."

CHAPTER 22

Japheth had fixed her ceiling and hadn't wanted to stay for coffee or to just hang around like he usually did. Jane figured it was because he was going home in a few days. What was the point of getting too close to each other if he was leaving so soon?

With Tillie asleep, Jane was settling down with a cup of tea when a knock sounded on her door. She glanced at the clock as though that would tell her who it might be. It was five o'clock. Miranda had already picked up her order and it wouldn't be her back again. She didn't know anyone who knocked that loud. She opened the door to see Officer Davies. Her heart lurched as she fevently hoped he wasn't there to arrest her. "Yes?"

"I've got an update on Scott Crittenden's murder."

She clutched her throat. "Yes?"

"We've made an arrest."

"You have?"

He nodded and for the first time she saw a hint of a smile on his severe face. "After we arrested him, he confessed everything."

"Who was it?"

"One of his brothers."

"Really? His own brother? Why did he do it?"

"They'd always had a heated relationship. Scott Crittenden allegedly raped his sister-in-law some years ago and when she told her husband, he went right over to his brother's apartment and the altercation took place."

"That's horrible. I wasn't the only one he did it to, then."

"It appears so."

"I'm totally in the clear?" she asked him.

"Yes, as I said, we have a confession that supports the evidence we collected at the scene."

She held her head and tears ran down her face. Her worries were over. "That explains why the family's not trying to take custody of Tillie."

He looked at her sympathetically. "Will you be okay? Do you want us to call anyone?"

"No, thank you. We'll be fine."

When they left, she sat down on the couch and cried with relief. Before all this had happened, she felt sorry for herself every day and thought her life was dreadful. All this had shown her just how bad things could've gotten.

Jane wanted to run over to Japheth and tell him she was in the clear, but considering his strange demeanor earlier, she stayed away. She'd tell him when she saw him at the meeting the very next day.

WANTING to tell Japheth her news, Jane got a ride to the meeting with Adam and Japheth instead of asking Wendy's family.

"See? I told you it would all work out in the end."

Jane nodded. "You did keep saying that."

When they got to the house where the meeting was being held, Jane saw her mother outside the house.

Japheth stood beside her while Adam secured the buggy. "Now's your chance to talk."

"I'll try." Jane nodded, left Japheth, and with Tillie

in her arms, walked over to her mother. When she drew close, they made eye contact.

"Hello, *Mamm*."

"Hello, Jane."

"All's good. I'm in the clear. They're not going to take Tillie away from me."

"That's good." As usual, her mother avoided looking directly into her face.

"*Mamm*, how come you never look at me anymore?"

Her mother glanced at her and looked away. "We said all we had to say a long time ago."

"Why have you deserted me? I'm still your *dochder*."

Her father walked over. "What are you upsetting your *mudder* about, Jane?"

"I came to tell her the good news. Those people aren't going to try to take Tillie away from me now."

"*Gut.* You can raise her yourself just how you always wanted, but you must leave your *mudder* and me out of it."

"She's your *grosskinn*. Don't you care about that?"

Her father rubbed his dark beard. "You made your choices a long time ago, Jane."

"I didn't choose this. I didn't choose any of this."

Her parents looked around about them when she

raised her voice. That's all they cared about, what other people thought about them. They walked away, leaving her standing there, holding onto Tillie. They had no love for her and they had no love for their granddaughter. At that moment, Jane knew they would never change. Tears rolled down her face and she knew she couldn't go to the meeting and face everyone.

One part of her life was under control, but she'd always be looked down upon for something that had been out of her control. She shook her head. Where was the forgiveness? The bishop and his family had been good to her at least, and they couldn't help the attitudes of the rest of them. If she told the bishop how she felt about her treatment, he might say something and make matters worse. It was best to let things be.

Since she'd come there with Adam and Japheth, she had to tell them she was leaving. She made her way to the door of the house and got Japheth's attention.

He walked over to her. "The talk with your *mudder* didn't do any good?"

"*Nee*. I just had a bad and horrible conversation with both my parents. I can't stay here. I'm about to cry and then I won't be able to stop. I just wanted to tell you that Tillie and I are going home."

"How?"

"We're walking. It's not that far."

"All the same, you can't walk home carrying Tillie all that way. She's far too heavy for that. I'll take you home and then come back."

"You can't."

"I can. I'll tell Adam where I'm going. No one will miss me."

Japheth was wrong; all the girls would miss him, but he didn't seem to know that. "*Denke*, Japheth."

"Go and wait in the buggy."

She turned around and headed to the buggy while he went back into the house. Good friends like Japheth and his grandfather and Wendy's family were even more precious when everyone else gave her the cold shoulder. They were her idea of what real Christians should be.

Just when she and Tillie had gotten comfortable in the buggy, Japheth jumped into the driver's seat.

"The bishop was probably going to announce that you're leaving soon, and he'll look around and you won't be anywhere," Jane said.

"You can't do much about that. Anyway, it's

embarrassing when that happens. I don't like everyone looking at me."

"I know, it's embarrassing, isn't it?"

"Their way of being friendly, I guess." He glanced over at her and she nodded. "Looks like Tillie's going to sleep," he said.

"She always goes to sleep in the buggy. It's the clip-clopping or the rocking."

"It used to put me to sleep when I was a kid too." When they got to the house, he said, "Do you want me to stay with you? I don't like leaving you alone when you're upset."

"You can't. That would look dreadful. You'd miss the meeting and then they'd find out you were here at my place." She shook her head. "Not good for your reputation."

"Or yours."

She shrugged and felt like saying it wouldn't change hers, but she didn't want to sound too depressing all the time. "*Denke* for bringing us home. I really appreciate it. Maybe I can return all these favors one day."

"Just bake me a cupcake, or twelve, since the batch always has to be divisible by twelve."

She laughed. "You actually listen to what I say."

"I do."

"*Denke* again." She wished he could stay with her all day, or at least for a few hours. When she and Tillie were clear of the buggy, he gave her a big smile before he moved his horse forward.

She watched from the porch as the buggy headed back down the driveway to meet the road. "And there he goes, Tillie." Tillie rested her head on her mother's shoulder. "The young women won't leave him alone. He'll find a *fraa* as easy as anything. He'd have a girlfriend by the end of the week if he weren't going home." Tillie yawned. "Am I bothering you?" Tillie stuck her thumb in her mouth and closed her eyes. "I must be really boring."

The only thing Jane was thinking about was all the girls who'd flock around Japheth, especially when they learned he was leaving soon. This would be their last chance with him.

CHAPTER 23

*T*he next morning, Jane opened her front door to Japheth.

"Jane, I've come to tell you I'm leaving on Tuesday."

She stared at him. It served her right for wondering if something might come of their relationship. Being married to her was most likely the last thing on his mind.

"Aren't you going to say something?" he asked.

"When are you going? This Tuesday, tomorrow, you mean?"

He nodded. "Tomorrow."

"So soon?"

"*Jah.* I've been thinking about you."

"You have?"

He nodded. "I think you should move away from

here. It would be better for you to have a fresh start somewhere, don't you think?"

She had hoped he'd been thinking about her for a very different reason. "I've often thought about it. It would be nice to be around people who didn't know me, and like you said it would be a fresh start. What about my business, though?"

"You'll find another Miranda, or set up on your own somewhere."

"Where would I go?"

"Move to Harts County where I am. I'll find you a place to live and help you set yourself up."

He wanted her to move to his community. That thought pleased her. "*Denke*, but things are okay here."

He breathed out heavily. "Why don't you take a chance?"

"On what? It'd be silly to move when I've got a place to live here and steady money coming in."

"I'll miss you."

She didn't know what to say, but she couldn't stop smiling. "Stay longer then."

"Adam's told me he's fine on his own."

"That's right. He's kicking you out."

Japheth nodded, and the dimples appeared in his

cheeks. She wanted to throw her arms around him and beg him to stay.

"I'll say a quick goodbye tomorrow morning before I go."

That's it? She was disappointed. Where was the celebration he'd talked about? "Okay."

He turned and walked away.

"What time are you leaving?" she called out.

"Eight in the morning," he yelled over his shoulder.

She hoped he liked her, but surely he would've asked her out or taken her and Tillie out somewhere —on a date, or something.

In bed that night, Jane tossed and turned, wanting Japheth to change his mind and stay.

~

AT EIGHT THE NEXT MORNING, Jane was ready and waiting to say goodbye.

She saw him from the kitchen window in his hat and black coat, making his way to her door.

After she'd straightened her prayer *kapp* and smoothed down her dress, she opened the door to his smiling face.

"You're really going?"

"Were you hoping I'd change my mind?"

"*Jah.* I was. Do you remember the reason you told me you were here? It wasn't to watch over Adam."

"You mean my *mudder* wanting me to find a *fraa?*"

"That's right, and you haven't done that yet. She'll be disappointed."

He held up his hand. "Ah, I said that's what *she* wanted."

"And you want something different?"

He looked down at the ground and then looked back up at her. "The thing is, I don't want to marry just anyone. I have to be certain."

"Of course." She remembered him saying people had said that he was fussy.

"And, I'm not sure what love feels like, to be honest with you."

There it was. He couldn't have said it any plainer. "I hope you find … whatever it is you want."

"Goodbye, Jane." He looked over her shoulder. "Where's Tillie?"

"Still asleep."

"Say goodbye to her for me?"

"I will."

They both looked over when they heard the taxi heading to the house.

"Here's my ride. Look after yourself, Jane. It was

good to meet you. I won't say I'll write because I'm not into all that."

Jane nodded. "I might see you again one day."

"You never know." He walked two steps away, stopped, and then turned back around. "Why were you asking me all that just now?"

"All what?"

"About the reason I came here."

She couldn't tell him she liked him because he'd as good as told her he didn't feel the same. Jane just shrugged.

He walked closer. "Why did you ask, Jane?"

"I just want you to … Everyone deserves love—to find that special person who will love them and only them."

"Is that what you want?"

His question caught her off guard. *"Jah,* I'd like that."

"I hope you find what you're looking for too, Jane."

"What about you?"

He tipped back his hat just slightly. "I'm not sure that love, as you describe it, is real. Love is a decision. It could be that you make a decision about a person and then stick with it."

She wanted to ask him if that were the case, why

had he come there to find a wife and why hadn't he found one by now in his community? It was as though he wanted to believe love between a man and a woman could be real and special.

The taxi beeped and Japheth turned around and walked away, leaving Jane to wonder when, and if, she'd ever see him again. He collected his suitcase by Adam's porch, got into the taxi, and before she knew it the taxi was heading away.

When the taxi was out of sight, she closed the door. Japheth had made her believe in love again. Maybe one day their paths would cross, or maybe God had brought him into her life to give her hope. Until she saw him again, she'd do her best to put him out of her mind.

~

IT WAS five days later when Jane opened her front door to take cupcakes to Adam when she nearly ran smack-bang into someone standing at the door. He had his hand up just about to knock. "Japheth!"

He stood there, smiling down at her, and then he nodded toward what he held in his hands. It was a white cake box. "Another peace-offering."

She laughed. "What are you doing here?"

"Can I come in?"

"*Jah*." She stepped back inside and placed the plate of cupcakes on a nearby table. "What are you doing back here?"

"I couldn't stop thinking about you."

Her whole body tingled. "Really?"

He nodded. "Every time I look at a cake, which seemed to be every few minutes."

She giggled at him. "Oh, you got hungry, so you came back?"

"*Nee*, Jane." He stepped forward, still holding his white box, and looked down into her eyes. "I came back to convince you to marry me."

Jane burst out laughing and then looked at his face to see that he was totally serious. "You want to marry me?"

His dimples made an appearance. "Only to help you out, that's all."

She looked into his blue eyes. "Japheth, I think you're in love with me."

"I told you I don't believe in that kind of stuff."

"It's kind of you to offer to help me out, but I can't marry a person unless someone—unless that person—is in love with me." She went to walk around him, but he balanced the box in one hand and took hold of her hand with the other.

"What's love? It's just a word," he said.

After she had glanced down at their hands touching, she looked up into his face. "Love is everything. Love is commitment, understanding, trust, giving of oneself …"

"Stop it! You're making me sick to my stomach. All right. I'm in love with you, Jane. Satisfied?"

She wrapped her arms around him and hugged him as tight as she could and the box squashed between them. Slowly, he placed his arms around her waist and while she buried her face in his chest, he encircled her with his arms.

"I love you too," she said softly.

"Be quiet. I'm figuring out where we'll live, and all that."

She stepped away and the squashed cake box fell on the floor. They both ignored it.

"If we're going to be married, you'll have to stop telling me to be quiet," Jane said. "It's simply unacceptable."

"You started the whole 'be quiet' business way back when we first met."

She giggled. "Then I'll be the one to finish it. No more telling each other to be quiet, okay?"

He nodded. "Done." With his foot, he moved the squashed cake and box out of the way, pulled her back into his arms, and rested his head gently on the top of hers. "I do love you, Jane whatever your last name is. You never told me your last name, do you know that?"

"You never even told me your first name. I had to hear it from someone else."

They both laughed.

"I'll be a good *vadder* to Tillie."

"I know you will." She closed her eyes and wanted to stay in his arms like that forever. God had sent her the only man in the world who understood her, and for that, she would always be thankful.

"Will you come back to Harts County with me? We'll make our home there."

"I'd like that very much. In Harts County, no one would know about my past, and I'll blend in and be the same as everyone else."

"Tell me you'll never be like everyone else. I like you just the way you are."

She pulled back and looked into his eyes. "And how's that?"

"Short-tempered, a little annoying, bossy—"

"Okay. That'll do."

"Is that a new version of telling me to be quiet?" he asked.

"I'd never say that because you'd never be quiet."

"If you don't stop talking, I'll have to kiss you."

She smiled, and said, "Right here, right now—"

He lowered his lips onto hers and kissed her gently.

~

JANE AND JAPHETH were married in Harts County three months later. Adam attended their wedding along with Wendy and her family. Jane's family didn't come to her wedding, but Jane still hoped that things between them might somehow mend one day. No longer did Jane keep up her frantic pace of making a living because Japheth worked hard and made enough to support the three of them. That didn't stop Jane from opening a small cupcake and coffee shop at the farmers market, even though they soon had another little girl, and then a third one.

Now that Jane had the life she'd always wanted, she had the strength to help others, as the handful of people had been there to help her.

Wendy accepted Jane's offer of employment, and her decision to make the move to Harts County was helped along by a handsome cousin of Japheth's.

When Adam grew frail in his advancing years, Jane and Japheth's convinced him to live in the *gross-*

daddi haus that they'd built onto their *haus* for him. That way he'd be close, but still be independent.

Jane was grateful to God for sending her a husband even though she had never thought to ask. If she had, she would've asked for one who made her laugh, a man exactly like Japheth.

The End

Thank you for your interest in The Amish Single Mother.

If you would like to receive email alerts when Samantha releases a new book, add your email below.
Click here to add your email.

Other Books in the AMISH MISFITS series:
Book 1 The Amish Girl Who Never Belonged
Book 2 The Amish Spinster
Book 3 The Amish Bishop's Daughter

ETTIE SMITH AMISH MYSTERIES (Cozy Mystery series)

Book 1 Secrets Come Home

Book 2 Amish Murder

Book 3 Murder in the Amish Bakery

Book 4 Amish Murder Too Close

Book 5 Amish Quilt Shop Mystery

Book 6 Amish Baby Mystery

Book 7 Betrayed

Book 8 Amish False Witness

Book 9 Amish Barn Murders

Book 10 Amish Christmas Mystery

Book 11 Who Killed Uncle Alfie?

AMISH SECRET WIDOWS' SOCIETY (Cozy Mystery Series)

Book 1 The Amish Widow

Book 2 Hidden

Book 3 Accused

Book 4 Amish Regrets

Book 5 Amish House of Secrets

Book 6 Amish Undercover

Book 1 The Amish Nanny

Book 2 The Amish Maid

Book 3 A Rare Amish Maid

Book 4 In My Sister's Shadow

Book 5 Change of Heart

Book 6 Game of Love

Book 7 Amish Life of Lies

AMISH ROMANCE SECRETS

Book 1 A Simple Choice

Book 2 Annie's Faith

Book 3 A Small Secret

Book 4 Ephraim's Chance

Book 5 A Second Chance

Book 6 Choosing Amish

AMISH WEDDING SEASON

Book 1 Impossible Love

Book 2 Love at First

Book 3 Faith's Love

Book 4 The Trials of Mrs. Fisher

Book 5 A Simple Change

WESTERN MAIL ORDER BRIDES

Book 1 Mail Order Bride: Deception

Book 2 Mail Order Bride: Second Choice

Book 3 Mail Order Bride: Revenge

Book 4 Widowed and Expecting: Mail Order Bride

Book 5 Mail Order Bride: Too Good For The Doctor

WILD WEST FRONTIER BABIES

Book 1 Mail Order Bride: The Rancher's Secret Baby

Book 2 The Nursemaid's Secret Baby

Stand Alone Novella:

Marry by Christmas (Western Romance)

ABOUT THE AUTHOR

Samantha Price is a best selling author who knew she wanted to become a writer at the age of seven, while her grandmother read to her Peter Rabbit in the sun room. Though the adventures of Peter and his sisters Flopsy, Mopsy, and Cotton-tail started Samantha on her creative journey, it is now her love of Amish culture that inspires her to write. Her writing is clean and wholesome, with more than a dash of sweetness. Though she has penned over eighty Amish Romance and Amish Mystery books, Samantha is just as in love today with exploring the spiritual and emotional journeys of her characters as she was the day she first put pen to paper. Samantha lives in a quaint Victorian cottage with three rambunctious dogs.

www.samanthapriceauthor.com

Made in the USA
Lexington, KY
28 June 2017